# Certain
# American
# States

## Also by Catherine Lacey

*Nobody Is Ever Missing*
*The Answers*

# Certain American States

Stories

## Catherine Lacey

GRANTA

Granta Publications, 12 Addison Avenue, London W11 4QR

First published in Great Britain by Granta Books, 2018
First published in the United States by Farrar, Straus and Giroux,
New York, in 2018

Grateful acknowledgment is made to the following publications, in which these
stories originally appeared, in slightly different form: *Oxford American* ("ur heck
box"); *BOMB* ("Certain American States"); *Harper's Magazine* ("Violations" and
"Because You Have To"); *Electric Literature* and *The Atlas Review* ("The Healing
Center"); *Granta* ("Small Differences"); *The Sewanee Review* ("Family Physics");
and *Tin House* ("The Grand Claremont Hotel").

Grateful acknowledgment is also made to Annie Baker for permission to
use an excerpt from *Circle Mirror Transformation*.

A CIP catalogue record for this book is available from the British Library.

1 3 5 7 9 10 8 6 4 2

ISBN 978 1 78378 220 8
eISBN 978 1 78378 222 2

Designed by Abby Kagan

Offset by M Rules

Printed and bound by CPI Group (UK) Ltd, Croydon, CR0 4YY

www.granta.com

*For*
*Emily, Eric, & Jin*

LAUREN:  Hey. Um. This is kind of weird—but do you ever wonder how many times your life is gonna end?

*(Another Silence.)*

SCHULTZ:  Uh . . . I'm not sure I know what you—
LAUREN:  Like how many people you're . . . like how many times your life is gonna totally change and then, like, start all over again? And you'll feel like what happened before wasn't real and what's happening now is actually . . .
*(She trails off.)*
SCHULTZ:  Uh . . . I don't know.
I guess I feel like my life is pretty real.
LAUREN:  . . . Yeah.

—Annie Baker, *Circle Mirror Transformation*,
Week Six, Scene IV

# Contents

# Violations

He had wanted to make sure she wouldn't write about him, but he knew he couldn't ask her outright not to write about him, since he was sure such a question would set off a lecture about how he was not within his rights to put restrictions on her work, and she might even tease him for being narcissistic enough believe that she was planning to write about him, and he would take issue with that word—*narcissistic*—a diagnosis she was well aware that he'd often feared his friends and acquaintances might have been, all along, privately giving him—and he would insist it was merely practical, not narcissistic, to assume that she, his ex-wife, whose last two books had contained many arguably autobiographical details, might choose to include some or many details that may appear, to some, to have been lifted from their complicated years together and their not exactly undramatic ending, but she would probably respond to this by saying it was ridiculous and childish of him to accuse her of writing autobiography—especially since he knew how much trouble such accusations had caused her in the past—and even if she did end up writing something that contained some or many details that echoed her life (as every writer did or had done at some point or sometimes constantly), she knew that he knew that she was not interested in writing memoir, and she knew that he knew that she was, as a reader and a writer, only interested in work that used the tangibility of character and plot as a method to elucidate intangible *ideas*, not to record a personal history, and even if she did write a character that somewhat resembled him she could never really write about *him*, the truest and realest him, because there was no such thing as an immovable, constant self, and even if there were such a thing she certainly couldn't claim she knew his, or if she did it was far too abstract to put into words, and anyway he had always seemed either incapable or indifferent to being emotionally vulnerable with her and even after all their years together she was still baffled and deeply hurt by the sudden revelation of his secret cruelty and the damage he had been capable of inflicting on her, so of course she wasn't going to write about him because she had clearly never known him—and no matter how many times he would try to interrupt this tirade (which would have, all the while, been increasing in speed and volume) he would not be able to speak loudly or forcefully enough to correct her original misunderstanding of what he had said (of course he didn't think that she wrote autobiography), but by the time she had finished her speech he would be too tired to say anything else, and his being too tired to make his case would be the equivalent of raising a white flag, a submission that might later double as his waiving any right to be dismayed by the inclusion of some phrase or plot element or character in her next work that he might recognize, whether narcissistically or correctly, as being based on something he had said or done or been.

So he never directly asked her not to write about him, as he estimated it would have caused more problems than it could have possibly assuaged, yet he felt unable to stop craving some sort of assurance that she would not write about him, or at least that she would not write about him in a way that was immediately recognizable, but the longer he dwelled on it and the more he talked about it in therapy and the more he talked about it in his head to the imagined company of his therapist for the rest of the week, the more he realized that part of his desire to make sure that she would not write about him was an even stronger desire for her to write about him constantly, a desire for her to feel his absence so profoundly that she was forced—like a child—to pathetically create a simulacrum of him and to spend so many years with that simulacrum that she would write one of those thousand-page tomes she'd claimed she'd never write, a book that fictively continued the relationship that she'd left—because regardless of whatever she believed about him really leaving her before she officially left him, she had been the one to technically and officially leave him—and in this book, perhaps a love story set in a lesser-known World War Two combat zone, her fictionalized equivalent would be a flawed, sentimental antiheroine and his fictionalized equivalent would be the sometimes misunderstood but ultimately valiant moral compass of the novel, and she would personally mail him a copy of the galley and just as he opened it to the dedication page to see his initials, he would receive a phone call telling him that his ex-wife had mysteriously and quickly succumbed to a rare but completely painless disease—as he didn't fantasize about her suffering, just her immediate death—and fresh with this news he would read her last novel, and in it he would see how she had finally admitted to being wrong about leaving him, and even if he had somehow misinterpreted the work—as she had often accused him of doing when he read drafts of her stories while they were together—this time she wouldn't be there to argue. This time he would be right and that would be the end of the story.

But she did not write about him and she did not die and he was often reminded of her not being dead when the mail came. Traffic and parking violations. Credit card offers and furniture catalogs. He would open the tickets sometimes, examine the surveillance photograph of her car running a red light, in order to be bolstered, to feel a little superior before calling her to ask, yet again, to make sure she had changed her car registration address, a task she said she'd completed months ago but clearly had not. But when he called she just said she was sorry, that she thought she had already changed the address and maybe it just took some time in the system and anyway he didn't need to tell her about the tickets because they were all linked to an app on her phone—just as everything in her life, it seemed, was linked to an app on her phone—so he could just throw the tickets and everything else away, just rip them up and throw them out, and he did this for a while until he realized that if he just kept throwing out the mail from people or entities that believed his ex-wife still lived at this address, then he might just keep receiving her mail for years, and he would probably lose hours of his life to receiving, ripping, and recycling her mail. So he began to write RETURN TO SENDER: NO SUCH ADDRESSEE in large black letters on every envelope and leaving them out for the carrier to take them back to wherever they'd come from and this did seem to solve the problem, though the catalogs and credit card offers continued to come, addressed to her but followed, uncertainly, with *Or Current Resident.*

He did continue to sometimes partially read the magazines—a few she'd written for and a few in which she'd aspired to publish. After peeling off and discarding the address label he'd bring an issue along for his commute to the university or let several of them stack up on the coffee table, and once the backlog was too large, he first recycled the magazines in which she had previously published, often without even looking much at them, not wanting to stumble across her byline, or worse, to catch himself seeking it out. He never expected to see her name in an issue of one of the magazines in which she'd never published, an expectation that had become so firmly rooted that he almost did not recognize her name beside a short story titled "It Wasn't," a title that, he smirked to himself, *wasn't* very good. He put the magazine down—he would, he thought, not read the story, not put himself through it—and he even went so far as to place the magazine into the recycling bin, but he felt immediately guilty for not being happy for her, as there was really no reason not to be happy that his ex-wife had found some success, no matter how ultimately inconsequential it was. So he let himself read the first sentence—

It wasn't the day he told her he was leaving that was the most painful, and it wasn't the day he moved out, or the day he re-moved out after half-moving back in, and it wasn't even the day they filed their paperwork together at the same courthouse where they had some years before—full of hope and endorphins—turned from two people who cared for each other to a single legal entity, and it wasn't that evening walk in the park that Gregory, a friend of his she believed was also a friend of hers, did not return her wave and abruptly took a left turn to avoid her path, and it wasn't even the day she got a string of texts from her soon-to-be former and grossly misinformed mother-in-law that alternated between passive-aggressive sorrow and outright rage, and it wasn't even that overcast Saturday morning when there had been a fire in the apartment building where she was renting after selling her house, and she had been shivering on the sidewalk across the street with her bed's quilt still wrapped around her shoulders and she realized she had no one to call but him and when he answered despite the early hour she briefly wondered if their months of separation had changed them enough that they might be good for each other again, but as she was telling him that she was standing barefoot in the cold street and had no place to go, she heard a woman's voice saying something in the muffled background of whatever his life was now, a life she knew increasingly less about, and just then her super came out of the building and the fire alarm stopped and the super told the weary tenants waiting in the street that there was no fire, false alarm, so sorry, no big deal, go back inside, go back to sleep.

It was a long sentence—really, way too long and for no apparent reason—and he remembered she'd once confessed to him that even though these long sentences came naturally to her, and even though they'd been approved by her agent and other writers and editors and critics, she sometimes wondered if they weren't a crutch or a limitation, though they did create a sort of momentum that she liked and perhaps there was something pleasantly flamboyant about how sprawling and nearly baroque they could become, and she'd said that Ursula K. Le Guin once wrote that Ernest Hemingway would have rather died than have syntax, and she liked that, and she liked her syntax, but she liked Hemingway too, and though she was confident in her work she also doubted she had the nerve or ability to write those sorts of bullet sentences, those quick little school-of-fish sentences, and shouldn't a decent writer be able to choose a technique rather than have a predetermined technique that pushed her around? But perhaps all this sprawling was, she'd told him, the living heart of her work and she shouldn't question it, as it seemed to be serving her just fine for now, but she did still wonder if it was a limitation, a gimmick, and now here it was, her first story in this magazine she'd always wanted to be in and perhaps he was the only one who knew that she may have suspected herself to be leaning on a crutch.

Even that wasn't the most painful moment. No. The most painful thing in this series of painful things would come later, long after she'd stopped bracing.

A little dramatic, he thought. Hyperbolic. Whiny. Certainly no Hemingway. He put the magazine down. At least it wasn't directly or clearly about him. For one thing, they hadn't divorced at the same place at which they'd married and none of their mutual friends would do something so rude as avoid her in public and his mother didn't even have a cell phone and there had not yet been, unfortunately, another woman's voice softening the hard edges of the apartment in which he now lived. In fact, *she* had been the one who'd jumped immediately into another relationship and *he* was the one who'd sometimes heard another voice in the background when he'd called about her traffic violations. He picked up the magazine again, started the next sentence—another long one—but put it down. He wanted to be happy for her, but the truth of it, he felt, was that no matter how shitty he may have been to her, she had been much shittier to him during their separation and divorce and he just couldn't be happy for someone who had given up on him so quickly, after he'd only done and later confessed to doing this one terrible but totally human thing. It all made him feel carsick, or as if he'd just gotten off a cheap carnival ride, and how was it that nearly a decade could happen so quickly and in the end all you had to show for it was a stack of misdelivered mail?

He decided to skim the rest, just to see if he needed to actually read it, but skimming became reading and soon he was too far into the story to turn back. And though he'd first thought that this story had nothing to do with him, it slowly seemed that perhaps all she had done was taken the facts of their relationship, changed the setting, and reversed the genders—made the man the one to leave, made the woman the one who was left—and for a moment he actually laughed aloud to the empty room. He was *in on it,* in a way, and she was nudging him, calling up a little joke they'd had about how she was his husband and he was her wife, since she was always hungry and wanting sex and he did all the ironing and had a more elaborate skin-care regimen.

And when he left town—even for a weekend, or a one-night busi-ness trip—he would return to their house (*her* house that had be-come, technically, *their* house, a house to which she still referred sometimes as "my house," though she corrected herself when in his company and let the error stand when she was not), when he returned to their house (a house she'd bought only months before they met and a year before he moved in and began paying half the mortgage and which, over the course of seven years, he had often offered to pay in full when her income was unsteady), when he returned to their home after a short trip away, she had, each time and without fail, moved most of his things to more discreet locations—the books on the nightstand back to their alphabetized spots on the shelves; the toiletries in the shower hidden beneath the sink; his faucet-side toothbrush placed in a cup in the medicine cabinet; a pair of shoes beside the door stowed in the closet—as if his absence had made his evidence upsetting, as if to be reminded of his feet and teeth and hair while they were elsewhere felt some-how perverse.

Well, yes, he did remember at least once moving her shoes from the living room to the closet while she was away, an incident that sparked their first serious fight, which ended with her storming out and being gone for half the night, coming home near dawn, at first not telling him where she'd been, then confessing that she'd just been at that diner on Flatbush, drinking bad coffee and writing something she was sure was terrible, but by the next morning they had the good sense to make fun of this fight, both of them accept-ing some weight of the blame so it could be lifted, though perhaps neither of them actually believed they'd been in the wrong. In the story, however, there was no fight or storming out, just some silent begrudging during which the wife and husband had syntactically complicated thoughts about the other. As he turned a page in the magazine, a postcard addressed to her fell out. It was an image of the Eiffel Tower, the word *Paris* printed over it in tacky red script.

M,

Can you believe how much time is gone since Liège? Thinking of it these days. Got this address from your old roommate. Are you still here? Are you still there? I heard you are a married woman now. I miss you very much.

Always,
Jean Marcel

Jean Marcel . . . Jean Marcel. In seven years she had never mentioned any *Jean Marcel* and it certainly wasn't from lack of her telling him about her past. She lived in a near-permanent state of nostalgia, saudade—a real affliction—and she'd told him everything, more than he ever wanted to know about past lovers, past travels, her seemingly endless, darling past. But no Jean Marcel.

*Jean Marcel,* he said, staring at the Eiffel Tower, almost expecting her to answer him from the other room, and as he stared at the postcard, he thought of that drawing of the Eiffel Tower that had circulated online after the nightclub shooting—and how sad that a drawing designed for international social-media grief had replaced any actual memory he had of the one time he had visited the Eiffel Tower himself—and at the same time he was thinking of the afternoon that half of New York was reading the breaking news of the attack on their phones and he'd come home to find his then wife crying facedown on the floor, hysterical—there was no word for it but *hysterical*—and once she'd calmed down enough to ask him if he'd heard about Paris (though there was no mention, even then, of any *Jean Marcel*), he had not understood why she could be so deeply moved by this specific act of horrific violence and not horrified when the same thing or worse things happened in cities she had, perhaps, never visited. Vacation-based hysteria, he had named it, though he never said the phrase to her, as this was far enough into their relationship that he knew how to avoid the land mines between them.

But perhaps it had all been much simpler. Her hysteria hadn't been, generally, about Paris—it had been about this Jean Marcel character, specifically. His wife was still in love with or had been, then, still in love with someone he had never even *heard of,* and it was only after finding out there was a possibility that her long-lost darling Jean Marcel had been gunned down that evening in Paris that she experienced, viscerally, how large her feelings were for him.

He picked up his phone and called her and immediately asked, *So that's why you were so upset about Paris? This guy?* And she said, *So you read it?* And he said, *Well, yeah—do you mean the story?* And she said, *What else would I be talking about?*

*Well, actually I'm still reading it, but—*

*Still reading?*

*I was just reading it, but I wanted to ask you—*

*I'm not talking to you about it until you've read the whole thing,* she said, and hung up.

He flipped through the remaining pages of the story, taking note of the sentences that spanned a whole column, hulking blocks of grammatically suspect text so rarely relieved by proper punctuation. Well, he wasn't going to read the whole thing, on command, just because she said so. He didn't have to do that anymore. He closed the magazine, looked at the cover image and headlines, picked up his phone to look up their circulation numbers, estimated what an advertisement would cost, wondered what she had been paid, and tried to find some information on what a person might be paid for such a story, but while he was scrolling through a three-year-old thread on a messaging board in which several avatars made speculations about what they estimated to be this magazine's going rate for short fiction and whether it would change based on the relative fame or obscurity of the author, his phone rang and his ex-wife's name appeared on the screen, as if she could still tell—no matter how far away she was—that he was dicking around instead of reading.

*I'm not done yet*, he said to her.

*But I just wanted to say something first. The man in the story, the writer, he's not supposed to be you or me. He's no one. He's an idea. And the same for the woman. She's a bunch of words. She's not a person. Okay?*

*Fine.*

*So whatever you want to ask me about after you're done with it, it has nothing to do with you and me. Do you understand?*

He threw the phone to the other side of the couch and kept reading about this couple who live in a college town in Kansas (a state he was sure she'd never even visited) and the guy is a novelist and professor (typical) and the woman runs a dog kennel (random) and the woman only seems capable of reacting emotionally to things that happen to the dogs in her kennel or people she's never met, and the farther away a tragedy occurred from her the more upset she could become, a condition that prevents her, after she learns of a terrorist attack in a nightclub in Paris, from even being able to get out of bed, so the novelist has to use one of his few days off from teaching to care for all the dogs in the kennel in their backyard, while his soon-to-be ex-wife weeps in bed all day, and in between taking care of the dogs the man is dashing back to his office to try to write this story about a young Frenchman who is attacked one night on a narrow street somewhere in Belgium and as he begins to fight off his attacker he is filled with adrenaline and rage he's unable to rein in and he stomps his attacker's head in with such force that the attacker either passes out or dies—and the writer in the story relished the seeming inaccuracy and ambiguity of the Frenchman's memory—and the Frenchman flees the scene, splattered in his own and someone else's blood, and he tells no one until he tells his American girlfriend some weeks later and the young woman is so horrified that she immediately packs her bags and goes to the airport and as she boards the plane she is overcome with doubt over whether she has done the right thing in leaving him. And when the novelist is finished writing this story within a story he goes to his bedroom to see that his wife has finally gotten up and is getting dressed.

    *So your hysteria has passed, I see.*

    *Hysteria?* she asked. *How could you possibly use such a word?*

    *Okay, your . . . sadness, your very profound and debilitating sadness.*

    *But you said . . . hysteria.*

    *Well, you were in hysterics,* he said.

    *I was being hysterical?*

    He paused. *Well. Yes. In fact, you were being hysterical.*

    She knew there was something she should say, something about the patriarchal origins of the word *hysteria* and all of its iterations, something about Freud, something about the very obvious disregard he had for women and her suspicion that deep down—and not even that deeply, it sometimes seemed—he believed that men were humanity's default and women were a sort of unpalatable deviation.

    But she said, *Forget it,* and they did.

But after that scene the story took some weird stylistic turns and suddenly the woman is confessing to her husband that not only does she allow any dog in the kennel to lick her in the mouth, but she also had a special connection to one of the dogs that stayed with them somewhat regularly—Ross, the dog's name was Ross—and once she had let Ross hump her for long enough that she found she was getting some sort of pleasure from it as well, and after she told her husband this he broke out in laughter, sure that she was kidding and what a raunchy sense of humor she had. In fact, the wife continued, she was not kidding and in fact it had been happening with some regularity for the past few months and she had no desire to stop this behavior, she just thought that he, as her husband, should know.

And this begins a strange fight between the couple that ultimately dissolves their marriage and at some point in the scene the gate in the backyard comes unlatched and all the kept dogs start running wildly around the neighborhood and from there the narration moves more associatively and nonlinearly through the wife/ ex-wife's mind, and it turns out that she'd actually been lying to her husband/ex-husband about her special connection to Ross, but the husband, in tears, ends up confessing to having had an actual affair with one of his graduate students the previous year, an affair he had ended, something he wasn't proud of, but she, still unable to feel upset by her husband's actually betraying her, tells him it doesn't matter and she was going to give him three days to get out of the house. The story ended—

She went outside, whistled once, and all the dogs returned.

He picked up the phone to call her, even though he was pretty deeply confused by the ending since the story began seeming like it was about a woman who had been left by her husband, but it ended up being about a woman who lied to her husband about dry humping a dog, and what could that even mean anyway, and as the phone rang he realized he really did not want to talk to his ex-wife about any of this, and when his call went to voice mail—*I can't answer the phone right now, so please leave a message*—that meek little greeting he remembered overhearing her record several years ago, and as he tried to recall that bleached-out memory, all the details gone, he realized the tone had already toned and whether he said anything or not, he was already leaving a message.

# ur heck box

It had become such a horrible, lonely place, she said. And the wind! She swore the wind was worse than she'd ever remembered and the light just wasn't as yellow as it used to be and it seemed that even the people had turned rude and gas prices kept rising. Anyway, she was tired of driving and she wasn't partial to the new preacher at church, so there wasn't much keeping my mother in Texas.

*Maybe*, she said in a way that meant certainly, *it's time for me to move to New York.*

It was nearly midnight when she'd called. It had only been six months since everything. I put on my glasses and sat up in bed as if that would help me see the situation more clearly.

*What about Maude and Jackie?*

*You know, I don't think Maude ever cared for me too much. She never lets me take care of Jackie, not even now, when you'd think she'd at least have some sympathy—but she still always takes them to Lisa and Bill, all the time with Lisa and Bill. You know, I think she resents me for being single by choice. And that's really another thing, you know. You can't do anything in this damn town without someone looking down on it. Not a thing. You know what? I actually hate it here. I never thought I'd say that, but I do. I hate it. They're all conservative, self-righteous*—and she stammered here as if looking for the right mix of obscenity and politeness—*well, blowhards, that's what.*

I didn't know how to react to her plain-laid feelings. Prior to this call she usually managed to avoid or dull any colorful emotions, her mood always placid, beige.

(The only exception to this beige-ness was The Christmas Fight (as I referred to it privately (it wasn't even really a fight)), which happened two years earlier when I used the word *home* in reference to my apartment in Brooklyn instead of the house in White Deer where she'd raised us. *So that's it?* Mom asked, trying hard to sound pleasant. *One year away and you don't even call this your home anymore?* She was aggressively frosting the annual spread of inedible gingerbread men (*They're decorative*, she always explained) and though I'd actually been living in New York almost three years, not just one, I didn't correct her, just shrugged, to which she began shouting—*You were born and baptized here, lived twenty-six years here, have a brother and baby niece and sister-in-law and mother here, but now you think your home is some place you hardly even know—well, if that isn't the biggest insult you could ever say to your own flesh and blood*—and in a way, I could see her point. A few years, my name on an electric bill—it didn't really mean anything. (Then again, I'd never belonged in Texas either—I'd lacked the accent and felt uneasy about how far away the horizon was. Maybe it was the belief that I could be anything in New York, even my boring self, that made me feel so at home there. (But even that was just a theory. (I don't know why I feel so welcome in such an unwelcoming place.))) Raeford was watching a game on TV, one arm around Maude and the other resting a beer on baby Jackie while she slept in his lap. He glanced at the kitchen, but ultimately gave us the privacy of his ambivalence. *Everyone you know is here*, Mom yelled. *Anything you could do is here! If only you would have seen that and settled down with Daniel*—and though I never drank beer I got one, hinged off the cap, and had it rolling down my throat before the refrigerator could shut. I hadn't been raised for confrontation. She hadn't taught me how to do this. I took a long slug of beer and hoped she'd just go back to being herself, a former Miss Neshoba County who never let anyone forget she was voted Most Amenable for both junior and senior year of her high school superlatives (though I thought she must have meant Most Amiable (but it was probably true either way (and I wasn't going to be the one to correct her after all these years))). *But you just had to run off to New York to do God knows what, and really, any woman would be lucky to settle down with Daniel*—(and if she'd been braver or meaner or just more honest she could have said, *especially you*) but it was then she seemed to realize how unlike herself she was being (how unamiable, unamenable) so she stopped yelling and nobody said a word until the dinner blessing. (*Amen.*) She never brought up Daniel again, but it didn't really matter. I'd already made it a habit to consider the way my life could have been if I'd said yes when Daniel had asked the question I knew he didn't even think was a question, just a rite of passage we had to go through. (You could see a marriage approach some couples in Texas the same way you could watch a summer storm churning on the plains, miles before it hit.) It was possible my life wouldn't have been any more or less enjoyable had I turned from person to wife, wife to parent, had I stayed in White Deer and parceled my hours out to a family, turned my mother grand. (A life might comfortably disappear into a well-worn groove between house, school, and grocery store. (All lives disappear one way or another. (All hours get spent.))) But as pleasant as it might have been, that kind of life also seemed—somehow—elsewhere, like a dream I could only watch instead of do. We were all surprised Raeford was the first to end up with the spouse, baby, mortgage—*Man alive, I would've sworn I'd be the one to get out*, he said during his only stay with me in the city. *And don't you fuckin' tell Maude or Ma I was dipping*, he said, with a lisp from the chew, *you hear?* But of course I couldn't have ruined their image of Raeford even if I'd wanted to. For so long he'd been something of a fuckup and now that he'd become (or seemed to have become) a Good Man, no one could bear to think he'd regress. When Maude told him she was *just a little pregnant*, some kind of man sprang up in him, dismissing the ex-quarterback who had been coasting on charm and Coors Light through community college. Ma stopped complaining about his longish hair, older-than-God Carhartts, or infrequent church attendance. Instead she cooed about her soon-to-be grand-baby and sent me meaningful glances. It was then, at the dinner table after Maude and Rae told us about their shotgun marriage, that I decided and announced I was moving to New York. (I guess I'd been guided by our unspoken sibling law of equal-but-opposite reactions: When I made mud pies in the yard, he played Nin-tendo. I went to church and he drank by the river. He grew a family; I fled.) *Wooo doggy*, Rae said in that elevated monotone he used to express both enthusiasm and disdain, *city slicker. Big-city gal.* Mom teared up, excused herself to fix us some dessert, then let the TV drown out conversation for the rest of the night. *It's just . . . so much*, she said as she shut her bedroom door, and she didn't say another word about my leaving for years. The next week we went to the courthouse with Maude and Rae like we were pay-ing off a parking ticket. Maude's parents brought their own copy of the Bible and Mom threw birdseed at the newlyweds as they walked to his Chevy. Rae slapped Maude's ass and said, *Wooo doggy, got myself a wifey*, in his usual way, but Rae doesn't say anything like that anymore and he doesn't slap anyone's ass anymore because he doesn't say anything or slap anything because he doesn't exist and this, I knew, was the real reason Mom now hated everything in Texas.)

It was June 26. Six months to the day.

*You can't move here*, I told her. *Everyone you know is in Texas.*
*Well, look who's talking.*

Mother's move to New York was just the latest of several problems
I had that summer. By then there were Rebecca's parrots, the Appropriate Behavior Rubrics at work, the increasing hostility of my
downstairs neighbor, and the small, strange problem of Maurice.

Maurice's problem had something to do with integrity or hon-
esty or setting something right, but I never understood how any of
it had anything to do with me to begin with. Actually, I don't know
what Maurice's problem was, but now that I think of it, his problems were probably bigger than all that. His deafness, for one, seemed
problematic, as did his reading and writing skills. Let's just say, for
simplicity, that Maurice's problem was me.

Rebecca told me it was best to keep busy in times of grief and
that's what I was doing when I met Maurice. There had been a late-
January warm snap and the whole neighborhood had flocked into
the park— coatless, delirious on their picnics, pale limbs exposed,
hyper children sprinting over yellowed hills. I had several hours of
science podcasts to keep me company on a walk, so I played them
one after the other, filling up my head, making no room for awful
thoughts. I was walking through a wooded path when Maurice ran
up beside me. He wore a backward cap and an oversized jersey and
motioned for me to take out my earphones. (There was a direness
to his face, I thought, or maybe it was just that jagged scar that
formed a *C* from forehead to chin. The knee-jerk fear that he might
try to rape, kidnap, rob, or torture me arose as a reminder that I
was still an anxious white woman from Texas, full of inherited
racial and social prejudice and the defeated expectation that most
men are packed to their necks with violence. (A more evolved part of

myself dismissed that thought (or maybe I just rationalized my fears away when I noticed this man's unintimidating build and remembered the statistical unlikelihood of a violent crime taking place in a crowded daytime park (or maybe it was just the heedlessness I'd felt since Rae died, that impulse I had to move toward chaos before it could surprise me))).)

I took my earphones out but he said nothing so I said, *What do you want?* Whatever he had to say or do—I could take it.

He pointed down the trail behind us, then at me, then at my shorts' pocket, back down the trail, then back at my shorts. His desperate eyes locked on mine.

*I don't know what you want,* I said. He made some indecipherable sounds, all vowel and *v,* then more vague hand gestures. It seemed he was deaf or pretending to be deaf or at least unable to speak, enduring some kind of handicap. I shrugged and started to put my earphones back in but he shook his head, pointed down the trail. I wondered if several able-bodied men could be waiting for this harmless-seeming bait to lure me in. I started to walk away, but he got out a flip phone, typed something, and showed it to me.

*it feel,* the screen said.

*It feel?* I asked.

He squinted at me, then at the words, hesitantly correcting them:

*it fell*

Immediately, I knew there had been an accident. (In the last few months I'd been avalanched by them: A woman had fallen down the stairs in my building, snapped her neck, and died by the recycling bins. A neighborhood boy had been smashed under a truck delivering apples. A distant cousin, Mom said, had stepped on an unseen crack in a frozen lake, then Rae, then a neighbor left a sticky note on my door asking if I could water her plants while she sat shivah for her mother. *it fell* fit into this world—everything was falling.)

Maybe an old lady had broken her hip, maybe his mother or grandmother, and he needed me to call for help.

*Someone's hurt?*

He nodded and typed something else on the screen.

*ur heck box*

I went at the words like a riddle: My heck box? You are heck
box? Heck box. What did it sound like—hegbogs? Hecho? Maybe
the *h* was silent? Eck? Egg? Egg box. Egg carton?

I gave up and followed him down the trail. A white guy jogged
past, his gait wobbling as he took in our unlikely pair. I felt embarrassed to see him noticing us and even more embarrassed that I tried
to signal, in a look, that everything was fine. Still—I was following
a stranger for an unknown reason. I couldn't decide if I was being
gullible, dumb, or something else entirely.

After several yards Maurice jerked still and looked at the ground,
peered into a bush, and looked both ways down the trail. Another
white jogger went by, gave us a look. Maurice exhaled hard and met
my eyes. I wondered if I could go now with a clear conscience that
there was no one to save, that nothing had fallen. He grunted and
pointed at me, then mimed putting headphones in while walking
in place, gazing up at the trees with an expression of despondent
terror. (I believed this was an imitation of me.) He pointed to his
hip pocket, then the ground, then looked at me, like, *See?*

But I didn't see. Maybe all the white ladies in the park looked
the same and he had mixed me up with someone else. (A woman
walked by us in clothes nearly identical to mine as if to confirm
this notion (yellow-y white sneakers, jean shorts, and time-paled shirt
(one meant to look borrowed from a man (but had, like mine, been
bought))).) Maurice kept looking hard at me, then took out his flip
phone and began frantically typing. There was something plasticky
about his face, something unbelievable about it. Wide forehead,
bushy eyebrows, an oddly small mouth.

He showed me his screen: *mayby the man had it.*

So there was no scam, it seemed, no accident, no crime. There was just something incommunicable between strangers.

I left him by backing away, then walking fast with the strange feeling that I had escaped some kind of harm. He looked dizzy with failure.

The summer I first started wearing a bra, Rae taught me how to fight. He was still a half-inch shorter than me but he weighed plenty more in muscle. Coach Stern saw him play a JV game and asked him to start practicing with the varsity boys, which gave him at least as much swagger as my figure had given me. Our bodies were announcing us as adults, ready for beauty and brutality—uniformed maneuvers and dresses that fit just so. During practice Rae heard some locker-room talk about girls from school and though he never told me who said what, he didn't like it one bit. He wanted me to be able to defend myself. In the backyard he waged slow-motion attacks, playing the part of a bad man in the darkness.

*Now if some jerk comes at you like this—what do you do?*

*Scream?*

*Naw, you gotta do more than that. Get him in the nuts. Get that motherfucker in the nuts, you hear?*

He taught me about pressure points that he'd learned from a karate movie, a certain way I could chop someone's neck that would make him pass out. But nobody ever attacked me. I'm not even sure a single boy on the football team knew my name. I had to wonder if Rae had made it all up, if he'd wanted to be a protective older brother even though he was ten months younger and I wasn't that much to protect. The closest I ever came to defending myself was when I went on a field trip to Houston and my mom gave me a little pink can of Mace.

*It's awfully diverse down there,* she said. *You just never know.*
But nothing happened in Houston. I came back to White Deer just fine and put the Mace in a dust-gathering dollhouse, tucking it into a tiny bed under a tiny blanket.

Rae still asked me to practice self-defense moves with him every weekend, and I failed to get any better at them until I realized they were more for him than me. After that my reflexes seemed to quicken. I memorized all the pressure points, could throw a decent hook. It seemed I could successfully protect myself if I knew I was doing it for his benefit, a kind of sibling symbiosis.

The months after Rae died I had the repeated impulse to do something inappropriate, something dangerous, but the only thing I could think to do was not get off the subway when my stop came. I imagined seeing the doors open on Thirty-Fourth Street and shut on Thirty-Fourth Street, then on to Forty-Second, midtown, and so on, and all the while I'd just watch the stops go, watch the people go and come and go again, watch the tunnels blur outside my window, and at the end of the line I'd exit the train as if it were nothing and I'd leave the station and follow the sidewalks until there were no more sidewalks and I'd keep walking until I found myself in a far part of the city and I'd stay there.

I thought about the appointments I'd miss, the people missed, the days missed, my apartment growing dusty, job unworked, e-mails piling up. I imagined my boss squinting at my disarrayed desk, wondering if my absence was (perhaps) the quiet evidence of my brutal murder, that maybe I was dead in my apartment, lying in my bathtub, disrobed and violated, my blood clotting in a thick black pool. Or maybe it was just the flu. Or an uncurbed addiction, a bender, a secret problem.

If I missed work for enough days and didn't answer my phone

they'd probably call my emergency contact, but the one I'd given was a former roommate I hadn't spoken to since I moved to my studio. Since I'd not yet had an emergency, my emergency contact had never been contacted, but I guess that's the thing about emergency contacts (that you never know if they're any good until it's time or it's too late (until the emergency has already emerged, and a contact is uncontactable)).

But I never did skip my stop. I always got out and went to work and no one ever had to call my emergency contact. The longer I fantasized about skipping my stop, the more I realized that it wasn't the kind of inappropriateness I was really after, so I began to imagine open-mouth kissing a stranger in the street, or doing an improvised soft-shoe routine down the center of a subway platform, or wearing a floor-length sequined dress to the grocery store. But I never did any of those things either.

I stayed the same.

Raeford was dead and I went about my business as if nothing had changed.

I did not become a new person. I did nothing notable. I was still just me.

The only thing I did after Rae died that I hadn't done before Rae died was tell people that Rae died.

*Hey, how's it going?* the barista at my coffee shop asked on my first morning in the city after the holidays and the funeral and the extra weeks I took off. It was the bitter peak of a pitch-black January.

*Fine*, I reflexed, then corrected myself. *No, not fine. I'm terrible. My brother is dead.*

*Oh. Oh my God. I'm so sorry.*

It was hard to talk about coffee after that.

*It's okay*, I reflexed again. *Well, no, it's not okay. He's dead. He's going to be dead forever.*

Then it was even harder to talk about coffee. We were still for a

beat until a Sheryl Crow song started blasting above us and he rushed
to the back office to adjust the volume. Usually just the thought of
Rae would lead swiftly to sobbing, but when I spoke about him in
public it was a novelty to feel almost nothing, not even that little
tremble under the face.

While the barista was gone, I thought of my brother's ashes blowing around the Texas plains, swirled by turbines, gathering on truck
windshields. (At the funeral Raeford's high school girlfriend, Mindy
Plunkett, had shown up late and wedged herself into the family row.
She had a big pink flower in her hair and she nodded at me like we
were having the exact same thought. (But we couldn't have been
having the same thought because I was wishing time could run
backward, make Mindy Plunkett reverse back up the church aisle
and never let her reach the goddamn family row and maybe time
could keep going backward, make Mindy Plunkett have never put
that awful flower in her terrible hair and then the days could keep
reversing and I could have gone with Rae to that barn party the day
after Christmas, or I could have at least driven him there or picked
him up in Mom's Honda, if I hadn't been as tired as I was, if only
I hadn't eaten that piece of yellow cake that was dry on one side from
being cut on Christmas Eve, if only that piece of yellow cake hadn't
lulled me into a sugar-induced stupor and if I could have gone with
him to the party and driven him home, or maybe he could have
driven us both, sleeping, into that pine tree, and if the awful smash
of metal and speed and sleep could have crushed us both out of this
world, then I wouldn't have to be here with Mindy Plunkett in
the family row with that fake flower in her terrible, gigantic hair.)
When she asked in a whisper where the body was I pointed to the
urn and Mindy Plunkett flinched as if she'd just realized that's what
dead means.)

Maybe I didn't need any coffee, I thought, but then the barista
was back, trying to mute his compassion, trying to just do his job,

to nonchalantly make coffee. Sheryl was telling us that if it makes you happy it can't be that bad, and I gave up trying to find a natural segue between death and coffee, just said, *A Red Eye, please*, but when he refused my three dollars, even as a tip, I felt ridiculous again. I moped in the corner with my free coffee and guilt, listened to a podcast about how geese use magnetic fields to migrate south for the winter.

Rebecca took me ice-skating in Bryant Park that afternoon, insisting it would be good for me to get out of my head, but midtown looked exactly the way my head felt: bleak and crowded, a few freezing vagrants shouting obscenities at no one in particular. It was an ugly Saturday and only a few holiday-bloated people were going around the rink, their waddling movements suggesting hangovers. I couldn't think of a worse thing to do while hungover. People made less sense all the time.

Rebecca was the brightest spot on the rink by far, her electric-blue scarf and yellow peacoat making her look like a bird that forgot to migrate. Her pale skin seemed even paler than normal, but in a way that was more fecund than pneumonic—and how did she do that, that healthy-pale thing? I never understood it. When she hugged me I saw a man in a respectable-looking herringbone coat throwing up at the edge of the rink. This was just the world: ice and vomit and rare flashes of brilliant colors. Some people drive their trucks head-on into pine trees and snap their necks. Some people wear pink flowers to funerals. I can't see how anything is organized.

We skated arm in arm because Rebecca has the easy demeanor of someone who grew up in a nudist colony. At her apartment there is a buck-naked family portrait, all of them so pale and so seemingly happy.

Rebecca didn't need to ask me how I was doing. She snaked one arm around mine then folded the other across her body to grip just above my elbow, knowing I needed to be held in place.

*The thing is . . . your brother died*, she said, breaking our long skating silence. *Raeford died. Not you. You have to keep living.*

Her voice was strangely ebullient, as if she said this sort of thing every day, as if it were her own chipper mantra—*Raeford died. Raeford died*. My ankles were bowing in, a sore throb in the stretched meat under my arches. I wasn't built for that kind of thing.

*You're still alive, so you have to keep living*, she repeated. *That's all you can do.*

I was too saturated with consolation from the funeral and wake to absorb what she was saying, but later I grew to resent this moment. *You're still alive* was almost as bad as *Let me know if I can do anything* and the empty glare that came after. I wondered how she would feel if she were the one dead and someone were telling her loved ones, *Rebecca died, not you! You get to go on living!* But I guess she'd just feel dead if she were dead and eventually I lost track of how I felt about her telling me I was still alive, still a life. While we skated silently, I thought about the formation of ice crystals, tried and failed to remember facts from that podcast about them. What was the point of listening to all these things I so quickly forgot? Once I learned a thing about this thing, I was often thinking. Once I knew something about something.

A child skated up to us, a red-faced little thing made genderless under considerable overbundling.

*Are you a princess?* it asked Rebecca. *Are you Snow White?*

Children like this always flocked to Rebecca as if helpless, a creepy inverse pedophilia. They gave her compliments and knock-knock jokes, presented their random shit as gifts—baggies of Cheerios, long-loved stuffed animals. She had a special way with them, but over the years I had stopped paying attention, stopped finding it cute. They never spoke to me, those kids, as if I were the unknown cocktail waitress clinging to the elbow of a celebrity.

Rebecca unlinked from me, and with nowhere to put my free arm, I thrust it into my tote bag, groping the apple I'd just bought out of guilt at a sad two-table attempt at a farmers' market. All they had were bruised, worm-dimpled McIntoshes, but after a sample-woman intercepted me with a chunk on a toothpick, I felt obligated even though it was mealy and acrid.

*Is she a witch?* I heard the kid ask Rebecca. Both of them turned to look at me. My bulky black overcoat, thick glasses, and charmless hair were not doing me any favors. Rebecca smiled, then turned back to the kid, trying to laugh it off. *What an imagination you have,* she said, but the little fucker kept a bitter eye flashing in my direction as it told Rebecca some dumb story about a snowball, but I wasn't distracted from the kid's knee-jerk contempt. I'm not blind. What a little piece of shit.

I wordlessly flashed the apple, made a witch face, and relished that kid's perfect terror.


Too embarrassed to face the barista again, I learned to love the watery sweetness of bodega coffee, the way it left me half-tired and inattentive. (I was less effective at work for a while, but it seemed like everyone was feeling especially February that February (even when a late spring came, no one could forgive the long betrayal of winter).) On the weekends I'd drink my bodega coffee on the little wooden bench outside, unless the hunchbacked man with the cigar was there, not just because the cheap smoke bothered me, but because he always tried to give me advice about how to meet a nice man.

*Everybody needs somebody. Aren't you afraid of being alone?* he asked.

*Right now I'm just afraid of death.*

*Aha! The ultimate alone.*

*Do you know how to get over that?*

I was serious but he just shrugged. *Maybe die?*

*I'll wait*, I said.

I'd heard a podcast about a tribe somewhere whose spiritual practices had involved, through intense meditation, briefly dying and coming back to life. Practitioners would slow their breathing until it was imperceptible. Their hearts would stop and they would just lie there for a while, dead, until they eventually woke back up and went about the rest of their day. I can't remember the exact details of how this worked and I can't remember the cigar man's name anymore, just his plaid pants and the polite nods we exchanged after the ultimate alone conversation, because, really, what else was there to say?

Then it was June and I started to feel like a new woman—not in a new-lease-on-life kind of way, more like a refinanced mortgage. I wasn't in a better place, exactly, but I could make my payments on time—feed myself, dress myself, be at home without crying. I had quit listening to podcasts. I felt I should try to get away with knowing less. But in the same way warm molecules move toward cool ones, everyone's problems started coming on, making storms.

Some alleged harassment at the office meant we all had to go to Appropriate Behavior Workshops and for some reason I was asked to be in charge of getting my coworkers to turn in the Appropriate Behavior Rubric Worksheets, which were held in great contempt. They all began avoiding me, took the long way from their cubicles to the office kitchen. I stopped getting invites to happy hour (or maybe that was because I never said yes). Rebecca asked me to take care of her parrots for a few months while she did some volunteer work in Nicaragua and their squawking woke me up at odd hours. My downstairs neighbor told me they woke her up, too, and she swore she could even smell them. An increasingly hostile trail of sticky notes ensued.

Then I was buying my coffee at the bodega on a Sunday morning, counting out my dollar in change, when I felt a tap on my shoulder. It had been so long I didn't even recognize him until he showed me his flip-phone screen.

*i fawn wat fel*, it said.

I was sick of complication and just wanted one day of peace and silence, so I smiled and nodded as if I were refusing, for the hundredth time, to sign up for Amnesty International. But he followed me out and showed me his screen again.

*i fawn ur heck box i am go get it*

*I don't know what you want from me*, I said, and it came out a little too loud and mean. He seemed to almost tear up at this (or maybe that's just how his eyes were), then ran down the sidewalk.

*Hey*, the cigar man shouted, *I didn't know you knew Maurice.*

*I don't. He's just confused.*

*Well, what'd he want from you?*

*Nothing.*

*Be nice to Maurice, all right? He's had it hard. He's had it rough. It's the least you could do*, he said.

*Fine*, I said, maybe too quietly, maybe so quietly I didn't say it at all.

I wasn't in the mood to be a person.

I'd thought my refinanced-mortgage attitude had been a signal I was getting better, but here I was again, just as terrible as I'd ever been.

I got in bed at eight that night and couldn't sleep. Maybe I could meditate myself to death and back, but I wasn't meditating. I was seething. (Was anger one of the approved steps to appropriate grieving or was that something from the behavior rubrics?) I seethed for a while, then I might have slept or died and was reborn when Ma called around midnight.

*Is anger one of the steps of grieving?* I asked after she told me she wanted to move to New York.

*If you need it to be, honey.*

I hoped that gentle tone meant she'd gone back to being who she used to be, that beige woman, the former Miss Neshoba County who had bootstrapped herself up when Dad left her in Amarillo, a woman who didn't complain about the wind or light in Texas, a mother who had only once raised her voice at me, a Texan who would remain a Texan, someone who could and would keep everything the same. I wanted her to tell me she was kidding about New York, that she wasn't going to change anything at all—but a few nights later she arrived, refusing my offer of the bed, saying she wouldn't be able to sleep if I was on the couch. I'm pretty sure neither of us slept because of the birds' intermittent squawks of *Becca! Becca!* and my neighbor's broom beating the ceiling under my floor.

*This is just temporary,* she said, *just until I find a place of my own.*

I started staying at the office late, then taking roundabout routes home, trying to exhaust myself so I could sleep.

*What do you do all day?* she asked one night, looking bewildered and somehow tiny, shrinking. She'd made an eight-dish dinner in my tiny kitchen, most of it involving corn: creamy corn salad, bean salad with corn, corn bread, corn-stuffed chicken, gazpacho polka-dotted with little white kernels.

*I have a job, Ma. I have to work.*

*With rent as high as it is, I guess you do have to work pretty hard.* (The girlish fear in her eyes reminded me of a memory I had of Dad before he left—how angry he seemed about the mail, ripping junk to pieces and making stacks of the rest, statements or bills or whatever. I feared the mail for years after, afraid of what responsibilities and problems would become mine.)

The weekends were somewhat better. I took Mom to museums and free concerts and we had some nice moments. She made us picnics for the park, where we'd end up napping, catching up on the sleep we'd lost to the birds. Eventually she seemed to stop looking for an apartment, though I couldn't bring myself to mention it. Maybe this was my life now. Maybe my mother just lived with me. And anyway, it wasn't as hard sharing the studio as I'd thought. She did all the grocery shopping and cooking, packed me lunches for work, and even started taking care of the birds, which had, in turn, chilled out enough for us to almost forget about them.

The respite lasted a week, until that last time I saw Maurice. We were walking to the F when he came running up, waving his flip phone at me with one hand, the other holding up his pants. Mom clutched her purse and whimpered.

His screen: *Ur hack in der got done*

He looked happier than I'd ever seen him, ecstatic, nearly manic.

*No! Just—ugh, no,* I said, hoping he could at least read lips, that he could see a no.

*What does he want?* Mom asked. *What's going on?* She leaned into me—*Is this about drugs? Are you involved in some kind of—*

*He's just confused. I don't know this guy.*

*He seems to know you.*

Maurice seemed to finally realize how pointless this was, how far away he was from making anything clear to me. He walked off, gave up as if none of this had meant anything to him. Then it finally felt so fucking sad, that he would someday die with whatever he'd tried to say.

Mom was still rattled but we went to the Met anyway. A few times on the train she asked me if I was in trouble, and I told her it was too stupid to explain. (I don't know why I didn't just tell her the story. (It felt like the most private thing that had ever happened to me.))

*Ladies and gentlemen, may I have your attention please,* a man on the train said several times to us, taking our attention whether or not we wanted to give it. He played some music from his phone and danced as if he were trying to throw his arms off his body.

*Is he okay?* Mom asked. *Is this all right? Do people just . . . ?*

*It's fine, Ma. He just wants some money.*

The dancing man went up the aisle with a cracked take-out container but no one gave him anything.

*Ha-ha! You guys—y'all—ha!* the dancing man said, as if this were all just a hilarious joke we had played on him, not paying him a cent.

*The rent is too high here,* Ma said, and I was comforted by her floaty, oblivious voice.


At the museum we hardly spoke, just moved in and out of the galleries, drifting by the artifacts as if we'd seen them many times before. *Wow, that sure is something right there,* Ma would say every twenty minutes.

We went to the cafeteria in the basement, bought plates of beef stew. In the booth next to ours an elderly couple were also eating stew and each drinking a miniature bottle of wine, and it was easy to imagine that this was what they did every Sunday for decades—wine and stew at the Met. That was their booth. That was their whole life right there.

*You know, I didn't realize how dangerous it is here,* Mom said.

*It's not that dangerous.*

She nodded at me, took this statement superficially into account.

*There's so much need,* she said. *And there's no space. Everyone's so desperate.*

(But what was wrong with feeling desperate? (I kept this question to myself.)) We forked our beef and chewed without looking at each other.

*I read an article about the best cities to get old in and it said New York was a good place. You can walk around. Lots of resources and hospitals,* she said. *Community and everything. So, I thought, well, I'll just move there. I'll sell everything I don't need, because after all you'd have to deal with all of it eventually . . .*

Her eyes drifted around the low-ceilinged cafeteria in a kind of awe. The man from the elderly couple was spitting a piece of something into his napkin, a shaky hand holding it to his mouth. I wanted to hear what the woman was saying but she spoke quietly and with some kind of accent.

*And I thought if I lived here I would need so much less,* Ma went on. *Everyone says that's good—living with less. And you could check in on me since no one would really do that in White Deer, you know. People just leave each other alone so much there and Maude is too busy and doesn't seem to care much for me anyway. So I thought, well, nobody really has to die so alone in New York. It might be a good place to get old and die—oh, goodness, isn't that a sad thought?*

I shook my head but I didn't know if I was agreeing or not.

*Well, you know, these kinds of conversations are never easy.*

With a mouth full of potato and gravy, I leaned away from my plate to push this food down my throat, to turn it into me.

*I just want to prepare you for that, you know, since you'll have to take care of all the arrangements on your own since Rae's gone and you're not married. But I don't think I'll be moving to New York, and in fact, I'm going to buy my return ticket for this week. So—I don't know. I don't know what we'll do.*

She pushed a pea across her plate, picked up a roll but lost interest in it before she could lift it to her mouth.

*Well! Listen to me—doing all the talking like this. Do you have anything you'd like to say about all this?*

There was something I wanted to say, something I needed to tell her. She put one hand up to her face and smiled as if this were some kind of teatime chat instead of what it was—cafeteria-grade beef in a stuffy basement under so many tons of the past.

*Don't you have anything you'd like to say?*

# Certain American States

I was one of those babies who look as if they won't survive to dinnertime, but somehow do, then become toddlers with the tics and nerves of a used-up veteran. Nervous about the television, whether it was on or off; nervous about the sun rising or setting; nervous over every knock at the door and nervous in the silence too. Leonard, that man who raised me, he is the one who remembers my nervousness. He once told me that on the first day of my life, on that still-dark morning, I looked up at him and he looked down at me and he knew and I knew and we both knew that we'd always dislike each other. My mother was such a good friend, though; he felt he had no choice. He couldn't possibly say no—not to a woman whose belly had watermeloned overnight.

*Godfather? Me?*

*Yes*, she said, *who else?*

Leonard always told it that way and I always thought, in fact, it wasn't such a good question, not even a little useful. There wasn't anyone even pretending to lurk in the shadows of that neighborhood of foreclosed homes. Just burned-brown grass and black-eyed Susans. He didn't know anyone else. She didn't know anyone else. They were just there, as if they had survived something together and couldn't help the affection it gave them.

*The loneliness of certain American states is enough to kill a person if you look too closely*—I think he said that once, Leonard did, while I was thumbing the photo albums again, trying to figure out what happened, how I got here. The loneliness of the trailer park. The loneliness of a warped Polaroid. The loneliness of the gay decade when I appeared.

But even though Leonard always disliked me, he had a stubborn bit of mercy, and for that I am still thankful. (If not a merciful God, at least a merciful godfather.) It wasn't his fault that she died while the ink was still wet on my birth certificate. We both blamed the other and we raised me in a cloud of resentment. He'd lost his only friend; I'd lost a whole type of future. Together we had gained something that neither of us ever wanted.

A week later a nurse removed me from my clear coffin and handed me, screaming, to Leonard. Despite his prayers to a God he didn't believe in, I'd survived.

As a kind of backhanded gift, Leonard told me we could speak to her and I believed him for so many years. We spoke to her aloud, giving her a summary of our days, what we ate, what we saw, and twice a year Leonard read my report card out loud. I spent all the school day thinking, revising, rehearsing the nighttime messages Leonard was careful not to call prayers.

Sometimes I'd ask a question and it would just dangle there, answerless.

One night I tried to kneel at my bed, but he told me to get up, that's not how we do it.

*But that's what they do in the movies.*

*You've been going to the movies?*

*I saw a movie once.*

*Oh, you did?*

*They played it at school.*

*That's not a movie, that's what they call an educational video. What kind of education they put in it?*

*I guess to kneel at night like this.*

*And what do they call what you do down there?*

*They call it a prayer.*

*And what have I told you about praying?*

*That it's useless.*

*That's right.*

*And that God doesn't exist.*

*You are such a smart goddaughter.*

*Can't I just call you Father since God doesn't exist?*

*It's not the same thing. Being a godfather has nothing to do with that God. God is just a sound made of a g and an o and a d. It's a good sound. That's part of the reason it's so popular. Everyone loves a nice noise. That and people don't want to die. They will believe anything on the off chance that it will help them not be dead.*

He put a brick-hard hand on my scalp and I felt all the pounds of him pressing down.

*Sleep*, he said, and turned out the light.

On the night of my sixteenth birthday, at the time when we usually talked to Mother, Leonard told me he had something to say and he wasn't going to say it to her; he was going to say it to me.

*I didn't ask for you. I had no part in your creation. I still cannot even understand how she had a baby inside her to begin with and she never even told me how. I was the only person she knew and she never told me what happened, not even once. Someone must have driven up at an opportune moment and done what they wanted just because she was there.*

That is what he said, exactly as he said it. I wasn't surprised. I'll even say, it made a good deal of sense because I've always had a box in my brain packed to the lid with vengeance.

That night he wrote me a check for two thousand one hundred and forty-three dollars, left the car keys on the dresser, walked to town, and never came back. I started packing my own lunches, signing report cards, and doing what I had to when the money ran out.


Decades passed and one night I answered the phone because it rang and that's what you do. That's what you do for the person who calls your phone. You hold up your side of the bargain. It doesn't matter how much I want to throw the phone straight through the screen door some days. I still answer it. I have always answered it.

This time it was a stranger, a nurse with a tiny voice.

*Sophia?*

*I'm afraid you have the wrong number.*

*Oh. Well. You wouldn't happen to know Sophia, would you?*

*No.*

*What about Leonard Brown?*

I heard that after a certain large earthquake or hurricane, a major river temporarily ran in the opposite direction. This was basically like that.


I had never imagined hospitals in the Dakotas, just acres of unremembered earth, but I suppose people must be destroyed there too. North Dakota is where he landed, where Leonard ended up and ended. Bald and in a bloodless haze he told all the nurses about the remote islands he visited, the mercenary armies he fought in, about beautiful women in dresses that fit just so. He told them my name was Sophia, which it is not, and in my pocket I thumbed the beet-dyed foot of a long-dead rabbit. I'd bought it out of a machine outside a bowling alley outside a town where I had run out of options. I looked at Leonard, my godfather, my once merciful godfather. I don't believe in godfathers anymore.

But when he said, on the last day of his life, that we needed to finish our dinner quickly because the last ship to Tanzania would be leaving soon, I decided to be merciful.

*Madagascar has been beautiful,* I agreed, *and also I find it strange that there are so many Italians here.*

His knees, beneath a sheet, trembled.

*How is your ravioli?*

I started to answer him, but then he broke character, looked at me, said my real name. Said he wanted to know how I was. Asked me how I was doing like it was nothing. Like he'd said it a million times. It took me a second, but I answered. Answered like he'd asked me a million times. Like I knew just what to say. He was no longer really the man who had somewhat raised me and I wasn't really the child he had raised. Those people were gone and now he was just a dying person and I was a living person and the dying and living have certain agreements about these states we're in.

*I am good,* I said. *I have a good husband who has a good job as a manager and I am a manager too, which means I am managing. We get juice in cartons so big it ferments before we finish it. We think this is good; this means we are on the right side of things. We know what I am, and he knows what he is, so that means I take out the trash.*

Leonard twitched again, a smile whimpered into a frown.

*Sophia,* he said, *what about the opium trade?*

*I can't tell you much, you know.*

*A comrade is always discreet.*

*I thank you for your discretion.*

*Opiates, as you know, are recession-proof.*

I waited patiently for the last few hours, most of them silent, his breath getting wintery, slow and cold. The nurses told me I should leave, that it could be weeks, days, months, but I knew what was going to happen.

He woke up suddenly, right at the end, and told me he was going very far away, to a remote location, in the Commonwealth of Dominica.

*Of course*, I said. I crossed my legs and shut up and slumped.

*Time travel*, he whispered, *they'll kill us if they know we've harnessed it. We must say we've never met. They could be following us right now.*

# Because You Have To

The telephone hardly ever rings but when it does, there is a good chance it is someone asking me how I am, and if I really tried to answer that question I suppose I could say I'm doing as well and as terribly as I ever have been, but if you stop answering questions, people stop asking them, and if you stop answering the phone, it eventually stops ringing.

A month goes by, you think—Oh, I've finally done it.

*

Yesterday I opened the side door because the dog was barking at it and I called out, almost called out your name, almost thought you'd be coming back now, that it was all a joke, ha-ha, and you'd be coming back, just like that.

Obviously it wasn't you. It was Wayne from two yards over, though it was dark so I couldn't see his face, could barely hear his voice over the barking. Wayne had found a loose dog and wondered if it was mine.

Wayne had the mystery dog—sand colored and fat—under one arm and I was holding my dog by the collar (that is, our dog—no—*my* dog, *a* dog, anyway, no one's dog, this dog you didn't take with you). This dog was lurching and screaming his dog scream and trying to get out the door. God knows what he'd do out there, dark as it was, afraid of flies as he is.

*Are you missing a dog?* Wayne asked.

*No,* I said, looking at this shit-eating dog of mine. I went back inside. There was only one dog relevant to me. I knew precisely where that dog was. In fact he was the only person in my life of whose location I was certain.

\*

Something my grandmother, who was a fascist, used to say was *You have to count your blessings.* Once I asked her *why* you have to count your blessings and she gave me a great smack to the ear. *Because you have to.* She was the most beloved fascist in my family, all of whom were flag-waving fascists.

Do I sometimes think fondly of her? Do I have a choice?

\*

A cat has been stalking around the yard, chewing up the tomato plants, hissing and clawing at the birds.

The dog sticks his head out his dog door from time to time or sits on the porch panting while the cat murders bird by bird. The dog seems delighted to do nothing. He licks the shit from his ass and smiles at me.

\*

You have been calling and hanging up.

I know it's you. The telephone rings differently when you call.

You can't tell me I don't recognize this. You have no idea what I hear, though it is so like you to doubt me, to assume I'm wrong.

It is so like you to not be here and to call as if to point out your absence and to say nothing just to frustrate me.

*

Furthermore, a mouse and her extended and ever-extending family have taken up residence in the shed, living on pilfered compost scraps.

The cat is uninterested in the mice and is set on his task of pouncing on birds when they land in the garden to peck around for a shriveled berry or worm. This cat wants to destroy beauty—I can tell. He is more than animal, he is evil, a plain enemy of the world. I wish him ill. I do. Almost daily I find a mess of feathers in the dirt. Some mornings there are whole bird carcasses left on my porch—eyes shocked open, brilliant blue wings, ripped and bloody. I have thought often of what it would take to kill a cat, quietly and quickly, with my bare hands. I have thought of this often. In fact I am thinking of it right now.

*

I set a small fire yesterday. I can't sleep and there are these fields near my house and I was out walking, no one was around—I wasn't even around—so I went out in the field and clicked my lighter in some dry grass and watched the flames grow until I could feel a warm glow on my shins. Who knows what became of it? Not me. I went home.

*What every crime requires*, you told me once, *is a decent getaway.*

*

This isn't a large house—four small rooms in a row, barely furnished, badly lit—and this wouldn't bother me if I didn't know what terrible thing had recently happened here, the thing that created the circumstance in which I could rent this place so cheaply, no deposit, cash accepted, no questions asked.

The landlady is broke and jobless, can't pay the mortgage, a single parent to two kids, had to quit working to take care of the older one because he, in a single week, threw a neighbor's kitten from a second-floor window, was kicked out of school for unabashedly groping another student in the hallway, and was later caught being molested by his own father, who still has custody rights until the criminal case goes through and they're not sure it will because the boy won't say anything and she's got no proof.

*It's just his word, and my word, and—it's like—it's like*—the landlady stopped for a moment, her mouth still open, still wanting something, wanting to say something—*it's like nothing belongs to you. This world, I don't know—it's like someone else has everything and you have nothing.* She was saying *you*, to me, but I knew she didn't mean *me*, but she did sort of mean me, and herself, and you. All of us.

The landlady didn't say anything for a very long time or what felt like a very long time. She swallowed hard and nodded.

*He's six*, she said.

\*

How long does an event stay in a room?

I have wondered this most nights, staring at the stained walls, trying to fall asleep, thinking of that man I don't know, that little boy I don't know, and whatever might have happened, which I also don't know. A few times I've tried sleeping in the yard, which was nice on the warmer nights except twice I woke up with a cat claw

to the face and if I ever catch that motherfucker it won't be soon
enough.

*

I think sometimes of the afternoon we moved in here—the dog, a
couple knives, a mattress, table, two chairs—and when you went
back out to the truck to get the last box (your shit, your box, I don't
know what was in it) you just got in and drove off. I went out to the
street where the truck had been and the fact that you'd just driven
off like that was still hanging in the air, a sort of post-firework
smoke, the sense that I had just missed something. Now that spot
on the street where the truck was, then wasn't, still has that smoky
feeling. How long will it last?

*

A family of raccoons seem to be living on the roof of the shed, just
under a low-hanging oak branch. They wash each other and seem
pleased with the way the late summer is going—me alone in this
house, the dog getting fat on the porch, mice running everywhere,
the cat's mouth dripping with bird blood. They waddle around all
night and sleep all day in a contented pile. I found another smash
of feathers in a mud puddle this morning.

*

The phone rings and I know it is you. It rings again—*you you you.*
It rings again and I pick it up and we both sit in silence and I listen
to you saying nothing and you listen to me saying nothing and we
both know the other is out there and we both know we are apart

and we both know where the past went, and we both know nothing at all.

*

I swear to God—this cat. Another bird left dead on the stoop. If I find this cat—and I don't care who owns the cat, whatever neighbor in whatever direction—I will destroy it completely.

*

I've been picking raspberries from the neighbor's garden before dawn with a flashlight. This, I feel, is not a crime. They leave them to die on the bush and I will not stand for it and I am not standing for it. I wear the camouflage jumpsuit you left behind. It reassures me that you are not just hiding somewhere. Sometimes I fling the jumpsuit across a chair while I'm eating a can of sardines. It's a lot like you're here. You'd be surprised how much it's like you're here.

*

I suppose I've started to become grateful that you left this dog, the only person I've spoken to in some time. I'm counting my blessings, as ordered. When I wake up I take him for a walk and when we first step into the morning air, I sometimes forget everything I've ever done, everyone I've ever robbed, every crime committed with you, and only then, for those few moments, do I feel I am a person.

I say, to the dog, to myself, *What do we even do out here?* I ask him, *Are you even a dog?* He answers by not answering, his tongue loose, his ears flopping, then I remember that all he wants to do

is fuck something or eat something and run around in circles forever and ever and ever.

You may have left this dog with me, left me with this dog, because
you believe we are perverse in the same way. That we deserve each
other.

\*

The cat is dead or gone or both. The birds are rejoicing, swarming
and manic in my garden, an entire town's worth of birds not being
killed or clawed. Someone has tacked MISSING signs on trees around
the neighborhood, taped them to streetlight poles and novelty mail-
boxes. I walked up close to one on a sycamore tree—*Our Beloved
Cat, RALPH, has been missing since 10/19. We are worried about
him!*—and a picture of the cat, the Ralph, scowling. I draw a small
cartoon penis aimed for his left ear.

\*

A bad week for the dog. Monday night I woke up to the sound of
him vomiting at the foot of the mattress, and Wednesday morning
I found him whimpering over a diarrheal shit spread between two
rooms. I stopped feeding him, thinking whatever poison was in him
would eventually run out, but he only seemed emboldened by the
fast and later that day he tried to fuck the side of a couch someone
had left on the curb. He started sprinting after chipmunks and
squirrels, barking until his voice ran out, digging holes in the yard,
knocking over the neighbors' trash cans in a rage.

One afternoon, exhausted by all his bad behavior, he was walking somewhat calmly beside me when a man passing us said, *Hi
there, neighbor! What kind of dog is that?*

*A horrible one*, I said, and kept walking.

Thursday night neither of us slept—he sprinted around the house, barking and vicious and I chased him, tried to catch him for a while until I gave up near dawn, slept a little while outside, wrapped in a quilt, dew soaked and shivering. Friday I left him tied up in the kitchen all day, put in earplugs, and turned on a fan to drown out his whine. I went to sleep early, but woke up to his paws on my face as he tried to fuck the inside of my bent elbow with a penis protruding like a terrible red stamen of some god-awful plant. As I threw him off me, he smacked his head on the floor, reopening a scab, splattering blood as he did a hunched run from room to room. In the kitchen I found the refrigerator had been knocked over.

I managed to get outside, slam the door behind me, and watch him thrash around the house, possibly rabid or possibly demented, destroying whatever life I'd made for myself in there.

I don't know what to do now, a state I am so familiar with it feels like my only true home. I had fallen asleep almost completely dressed. Heavy boots, stockings, a big wool skirt. No shirt, but I've got the quilt, though it's mildewy from being damp most of the time, or maybe that's just me. I wander the yard wearing it like a cape, only then realizing that the mice are gone and I haven't seen any of the raccoons in days. I can hear the dog yelling in the house— *Dog! Dog! Dog! Dog! Dog!* the dog says. I must find a way to be more like this dog and much less like him too, I think. Then I see Ralph's teal collar and some splintered bones scattered around the back of the shed.

Maybe being less like the dog is better than being more like the dog. But it's hard to say.

*

It's Wayne again, I see him coming toward me in the grocery store. I had managed to slip into the house and get my overcoat and wallet, without waking the dog, though I had forgotten to put on a shirt so I had to keep the coat on everywhere I went, lest I make a problem for myself. I thought if I walked to town I might find some kind of redemption, maybe a fresh juice, something a real person would consume, and this is when I see Wayne.

*We think you know something,* he says, *about Ralph.*

This just doesn't seem like enough information for me to form a legitimate response, so I wait.

*Wayne,* I say, using his name all nice like that, like people do, *what is it that you think I know about Ralph?*

He tells me someone saw me struggling with the cat and yelling at it a couple weeks ago, one morning, when it appeared I had been sleeping in my yard. He tells me he knows that I was the one who set the fire over on that empty lot and he put it out himself and didn't report me. I realize I may not have been making such a great impression on the neighborhood, that maybe I should have tried harder to convince them I wasn't all bad, smiled a little, lingered in the small talking people do on sidewalks. I've never been convicted of a crime but I have a convict's face, always have.

*Ralph,* I say to Wayne, *if that's even his real name, killed just about every bird that ever flew near my garden this summer.*

*He's a cat,* Wayne says.

*That much is clear, but the fact stands that he was doing legitimate damage to the local bird population.*

Wayne scrunches his face at me. *Now, what are you really saying? Are you saying you did something about this, that you . . . retaliated?*

*What I'm saying is that it might not be so reasonable for a person to be upset by the disappearance of a cat if the cat was a known threat to a more vulnerable species. How do we know that the birds he ravaged weren't endangered? And how do we know that Ralph's deflation of the bird population wouldn't have caused a spike in the insect population, which could have caused crop problems, famine, and so forth? How do we know that the overall good that came from his vanishing isn't greater than the good he may or may not have caused in the lives of his owners?*

My overcoat is a thick parka with a fur-lined hood. You got it for me, stole it from a ski lodge, you said. It was almost too heavy for the cool morning walk to town but now, just past noon and warm, it is fully inappropriate. Wayne is wearing flip-flops. As I explain the relative costs and benefits of the existence of Ralph or the non-existence of Ralph, we walk from the grocery store and into the parking lot, Wayne flip-flopping beside me, listening. He really is a good listener, that Wayne, and observant.

*Aren't you too hot?* he asks, pointing at the coat.

*No*, I say, putting the hood up, and just then, at the edge of the parking lot I notice the landlady loading her children and groceries into her car. She waves vaguely at Wayne and Wayne waves back. I don't wave at anyone, just watch the landlady's car reverse and turn and leave the parking lot and disappear around a corner. I am beginning to think she just wants to be someplace else, anyplace else, and will say anything and do anything to get there.

# Please Take

Everyone was talking about having less—picking up everything you owned and asking, *Does this bring me joy?* And if it didn't you had to get rid of it. Everyone was doing this, asking themselves about joy. It felt incredibly dangerous. I was afraid for the world.

I was staring into Adrian's closet. Pants. Belts. Shirts. So many shirts. More shirts than he ever wore, more shirts than anyone could wear in a life. The brown flannel, striped oxford, baggy cardigans—none of it brought me joy. Nor did the jeans and slacks smushed in the back, old, forgotten. I couldn't even ask myself about the thousand wool socks, the yellowed undershirts, the boxers, or that one decaying sweater I thought, perhaps, I had given him long ago.

There was one shirt, though, pale blue with tiny green stripes, paper-thin and soft—I almost kept it. Adrian had worn it, I thought I remembered, at a picnic. Someone else's dog was there. We never had a dog. After the picnic we had talked about getting a dog, but we soon forgot we'd wanted one and by forgetting that desire we realized it hadn't been so true. So we said. That had been years ago. Now all I had was this faded, worn-out shirt and a memory but the memory had to go and the shirt had to go, just as days and people had also gone, just as so many tangible and intangible things enter and exit a life. Heaps grew; the closet emptied. I felt oddly fine.

My neighborhood is one of those where you can leave all manner of things to be taken, leave things on stoops or flung over shrubs, leave household crap or books stacked on curbs, what have you, what has anyone—and passersby will take these things. So I folded the clothes in stacks and stacked the stacks on the steps, draped the coats on a fire hydrant, lined the shoes at the street, and left a sign: PLEASE TAKE. Two days, no rain, everything gone. Piece by piece, then a van came.

But Adrian did not go as slowly. He went all at once. Here, then not. That was weeks earlier, a month even, a month and a half. You know, time passes strangely in times like that. You look up and think, Wasn't I just married last year? No, that was five years ago. Wasn't I just walking down Arabella when a bird landed on some crepe myrtle, shaking white flowers over my head—no, that was decades ago, a childhood memory you keep close by for no reason. Well, wasn't I just in Guam? You were never in Guam; perhaps you dreamed it? No. No, I don't dream anymore. Well, wasn't it just yesterday, just yesterday, wasn't it? They call it mourning, I'm told, so people in it remember to get out of bed.

The neighbors, having noticed the clothes, asked me if everything was okay. Well, not all the neighbors, but one neighbor, Corina— she asked. Corina is old, all burned up and tiny, and lives alone in 2F. She often receives heavy, large packages—nearly the size and weight of a human body—and I carry them up to her floor. And when I do something like leave my husband's clothes strewn across our stoop and sidewalk, she asks me about it, asks me just what the hell might be going on.

I told Corina, *I'm moving on.* And she said, *Is that so? Good for you.* And I said, *You know, it's really fine. It's going to be just fine.* I nodded and she nodded. I asked her, *It's fine, isn't it?*

I thought perhaps she would tell me some great wisdom to confirm my decision to move on, to get it over with, to begin again.

*It's not fine*, she said. *Nothing is just fine about this. Can't you see? It cannot be undone.*

And she said, *Kate, you must know that death is not that which gives meaning to life.* And I told her, yes, that I believed I had read that somewhere, but Corina, having not heard me, continued on— she said, *Life is that which gives meaning to life*, so I said, a little louder, *Yes, Corina, I read that story many times, everything dies and knowledge is circumstantial*—and she, having still not heard me or perhaps just unwilling to listen, she said, *The human heart has the capacity to make enormous changes at the last minute*, and I said, *I know this well, Corina, I've heard all this before, I must have read it somewhere.*

Just that morning, Corina told me, she had been clearing off her desk. It had been months, perhaps years (*Who can tell anymore?*), and she had been going through the papers, the letters, receipts, tax forms, old postcards, legal documents, currency from countries she couldn't remember, a pocketknife, another knife, unsent letters, and eventually, she said, eventually she had forgotten what she'd origi- nally been looking for, and she worried that she had accidentally, perhaps, thrown this thing out years ago and she'd only just now realized she needed it. Only—what was it?

I told her I was so sorry, but that I had to go now and she agreed that she too had to go. She'd just realized that she'd left the but- termilk out, so she went to her buttermilk and I went to the park. It was spring so people had their legs out, and good-looking people had become, it seemed, incredibly good-looking people, and even regular people seemed aided by the light.

Habits were helpful, someone had told me—people were always giving me advice for this newly broken life—so the park was my habit, the way I was structuring my days. Habitual bench, habitual time of day. These little things will make life bearable, they said (Who said? I can't remember).

On the walk to the park I always saw a man smoking cigarettes behind that restaurant, same man who was always there, and a black-haired woman reading library books on a bench just outside the park, same woman each afternoon, and that tall, large-nostriled man with a little boy in the playground, same man, same boy. How many of them, I wondered, kept these habits for the same reason I did—like a single nail somehow holding up the whole home? I did not dare look at them too closely, didn't want to confirm anything, to catch a glance that felt familiar.

Returning from the park I would sometimes miss my building and only realize the mistake once I was several doors away, and sometimes I made it all the way to Lafayette, where I stood at the curb wondering where on earth I was or wondering if perhaps my home had been somehow taken away forever this time, and now I was all that was left. But I always turned and walked back. I went inside. I locked the three doors behind me. Once or twice I left all the doors slightly ajar, wondering if anyone might stop by, let themselves in, make themselves comfortable.

The last time I saw my husband it was nearly four in the morning and he had a plane to catch. We had stayed up late fighting about something, who knows what we were really fighting about (what couple ever really knows what they're fighting about?) but we had worn ourselves out—me shouting at him from bed, him shouting at me from the bathroom, neither of us even able to hear what the other was saying. Then I gave up, mumbled, and wept into the pillow as he sang in the shower, all low and throaty, some jokey country song. We were the sock and buskin, he and I, always understudying each other but hardly ever called to switch.

He packed a two-month suitcase while I was half-asleep, waking me up to do our goodbyes, cool kiss on my meaty face. It wasn't clear who should apologize or what for.

But in some wordless corner of us we must have also known or felt—this is the last time. So the apology kiss became urgent and more urgent, and it became more like an early-days kiss, like time had bent our love back on itself, folded it like a sheet with the end meeting the beginning. And the urgency built, became animal, and I heard his belt clang just before he pushed me over, pushed the sheets aside, pushed into me, and even though I don't usually like it this way, face in pillow, hardly able to move, a startling angle—it seemed just then that this was all I could bear. To be done to.

Afterward he stood there at the door, suitcase in hand, and he looked at me not like a man who was leaving but like a man who had just arrived, as if he had just come home and hadn't expected to find me here. He smiled, uncertain, in the lamplight, said, *Bye*.

I heard his band almost canceled the tour but couldn't for some reason, just took two nights off and hired another bassist. Adrian himself had been a replacement for a replacement, so it seemed they had been ready, all along, to replace him as well.


In the park one day a man, a stranger, sat on the other end of my habitual bench wearing Adrian's worn-out pale blue shirt, the one I almost kept.

*I almost kept that one*, I said. I didn't even have to turn my head to see it. My peripheral has always been strangely strong, though I'm nearsighted for everything else. Before us a half dozen tennis players darted and swung themselves across the courts. I kept my eyes on them, listening to every groan and gasp.

The man said, *Sorry?* And I said, *No, you're not*. And he said, *What?* And I said, *Why would you be?*

*I think you must have me confused with someone else*, he said, and finally I turned to him. Very quickly I could tell that this man was in a sort of life intersection. Not a crossroads, not a time where a decision needed to be made, but something like a junction in an old, unplanned city where ten streets hit each other in a burst and there is nothing but choices and no clear answers and no clear path, just chaos, too many options. Perhaps he had spent years of his life in such a place, wandering from corner to corner, wearing shirts picked up off the street.

*No*, I said after a considerable pause, *I'm not confused. You're the man wearing the shirt you're wearing.*

I slid down the bench to be closer to him, or to the shirt, or the past—it wasn't exactly clear. The shirt held this man more snugly than it had fit Adrian. A little gnarled and bursting, this man. He told me his name was Frank but that people called him Frankie. The hairs on Frankie's arm were raised, alert, so I patted them down only to watch them rise again.

*It was my husband's shirt, and now he's not around and you're wearing his shirt. Now it's your shirt.*

*You mean he's . . .*

I answered his nonquestion in a glance. We already had a shorthand, Frankie and I. It could've had something to do with the shirt, maybe. I reached out to touch the sleeve. It felt the same as ever.

*And you gave away all his clothes?* Frankie asked, and I said, *Yes, that's right.*

After a long silence Frankie said, *That's wild*, all slow and reverent. *You don't care or nothing? You don't want to hold on to them?*

I didn't say anything and he took that as an answer, nodded, looked back up at the matches being won and lost.

*I'm forty-three years old*, he said, *and I've never known anyone who died. Puts me on edge, you know? Even my grandparents, all four of them, still alive. Everyone's still alive. All my stupid friends, even though we've done such stupid shit—we should be dead, at least one of us, but— nope. Living.*

I didn't see why this was a problem really but I didn't say so.

I didn't know how it might work over there, for those still sipping pulpy juices beside a great pool of life.

We kept silently watching the people hurl themselves around the green courts, and I considered telling Frankie the story that Corina had once told me about that long white scar on her arm. When she was a young wife, she said, there were all these *temptations*, and she'd never quite managed to sweat out all those years of Catholic school, so she bent one edge of a coat hanger into the shape of a snake, held it over the stove flame till it was nearly molten, and branded herself. She didn't want to forget, she told me, how much she cared about doing right. Now there's this smooth white snake on her arm, keeping her out of trouble, perhaps, writhing there for at least a few more years. *I didn't know you were married*, I told Corina when she told me this, not knowing what else to say. *I still am*, she said.

I wanted to tell Frankie this story, I guess, as a long way of saying that a person can force whatever issue they want on themselves, but the more I thought about that idea the less I was sure about it, so I kept quiet. Light was leaving, and tennis players were leaving, and eventually I was leaving too. I got up and said, *So long*, to Frankie, went home, not missing my door this time, knowing right where I belonged.

A few days later Frankie met me at that park bench again. He was holding the blue shirt folded in a neat square.

*I don't like it anymore*, Frankie said. *Here. I washed it.*

*I don't want it back.*

*Just take it.*

I got up and began walking home and it's not my fault that Frankie followed me. He kept saying, *Just take the shirt, just take it back*, and usually I wouldn't accept a strange man following me home but when I got to my door I somehow invited him in. Wordless, he followed, and though I told him to make himself at home he just stood still and dumb by the door before lowering himself, silently, onto the couch.

I got us two glasses of water, adding slices of lemon though I never do that, had never done that before, and haven't done that since. We sat in the living room for a moment. He looked around. *Nice place*, he said, though he would have said that anywhere, Frankie, that's the sort of man he is, I guess, finding niceness in every glance.

I said, *Frankie, put the shirt back on.*

*Listen, is this some kind of . . .* But he seemed unable to finish the question. *Just what is it you're after?*

*Put the shirt back on.*

He drank his water, drank it deeply, finished it. He stood up and unbuttoned his shirt as if it were physically painful, as if he were removing a body part. He put on the blue shirt in a hurry then stood there all still and uncertain and my God, I thought he was going to cry, sweet Frankie.

*You must miss him*, Frankie said. *I can't imagine. I just—I can't imagine.*

He was covering his eyes. I looked at the carpet. I looked at the ceiling. I looked at the shirt and for a moment everything was perfect. Something had vanished and something had been found. I had found some sort of unfolding that was not yet done unfolding and it was golden hour and the light fell into the room like a gift for which I'd already written the thank-you note and could now just enjoy.

*I used to wake in the middle of the night and check to see if my husband was still my husband or if he was actually a sack of flour*, I eventually said, hiding my hands behind me like a shy child. *You know how in high school they used to give teenagers sacks of flour to make them not want to impregnate each other? It was like that except he was a whole human-size sack of flour that looked and acted like a human being but was really a sack of flour.*

Frankie said he understood me completely and I believed him. It didn't matter if I really thought he understood, just that I believed him.

*Did you know your fears become your life?*

I told him I had read that somewhere.

*No,* he said, *I am saying it to you now.*

*It's true,* I said. *I agree with you. I see the world the way you do, at least in this one regard.*

*How nice for us.* Frankie picked up and finished my glass of water, fishing the lemon slice out and absently ripping it to bits.

*I used to always worry that Adrian would die in a plane crash or from some undetectable illness or that he would be mistaken for some-one else and fatally knifed. Then he did die, and now I haven't stopped wondering if I worried it into being.*

*Well, it was going to happen one day or another,* Frankie said. *Not to be a downer, but you know it's true.*

He had a point, I just didn't like his point. I suppose I wanted to feel that I had known all along how it would end, that I contained some sort of foresight.

*How did he die?* Frankie asked, hunched over the coffee table, pushing the torn lemon rind into a little pile.

*I don't want to say.* Or perhaps I didn't know or couldn't remem-ber or perhaps it had never happened. I felt sure that I had never known a single thing for certain, but that couldn't have been true. I must have known something. I knew nothing's ever been written that can't be erased. I knew that every idea negates another. Every page I've ever read shuts some doors and opens others. Everything breaks even. And maybe I said some of this to Frankie, or maybe he was the one saying it to me. It's so hard to remember, to keep anything straight. Anytime I speak or listen to another person I feel there is a hand atop mine on a Ouija board and it's never clear who is moving and who is being moved and I think I'm always looking for the times that the pair can be moved by a third thing, something outside us, better than us.

Just then the door opened and Adrian was there, dragging his suitcase, looking weary from all the places he'd been. He said, *You left it unlocked again.*

The room was very still and Frankie stood there like a photograph of himself.

*Is that my shirt?*

*It's joyless,* I said to Adrian. *You don't need it.*

*Says who?*

The window was wide open and Frankie was gone, taking the shirt with him. He must have crawled out onto the ledge and dropped onto the stoop, which was a way I had also escaped, at least once in the past and perhaps again very soon—it isn't such a difficult thing to do. Still, I admired him for doing it, for doing something so simple as leaving.

Adrian opened his suitcase and all the clothes I'd given away were there, dirty from the afterlife he'd returned from, and already he was laughing, already he was smiling again, fine with being undead, coming home to the same home, staying, somehow, always the same.

I weep athletically almost every day and sometimes I cannot get down a city block without collapsing but Adrian is always upright and smiling and glad, so glad, so glad. It may be we do not live in the same world at all. Some nights I wake up and panic, thinking he's truly gone, for real this time, and I lie there shaking, all my organs going wild in me for hours until I roll over and see he's been beside me all along. I keep sleeping in the wrong places, I think, or maybe I'm just waking up not where I am.

# The Healing Center

Sylvia put her hands on her belly and she put her hands on her hips and she faced the mirror and she turned sideways to the mirror and she faced it again. I lowered my hands from my chest and put them on my hips too and looked into the mirror at the opposite of Sylvia and at the opposite of me, at all the flesh and hair and shapes we were living in.

*Why do we look like this?* Sylvia asked, so I asked Sylvia, *Why do we look like what?* and Sylvia said, *Like women? Why are we women?*

I looked at Sylvia's body in the mirror and I looked at my body in the mirror and I remembered that my skin is the color that panty-hose companies mean when they say *nude* and Sylvia's skin is not that color. Sylvia is an ample woman and she is the right kind of ampleness, by which I mean she has been strategically engineered by God or whatever to cause earthshaking want in people, the kind of want that leads people to stay up all night, hostage.

*I don't know*, Sylvia said. *Never mind.*

Sylvia was doing a lot of never-minding back then, so much never-minding that it became unclear if she minded anything at all anymore, or if she minded her own mind or even my mind, or anything that was mine. She'd spent the week cutting her bangs slanted and balancing grapes on her belly button and letting pots of porridge cook to soot on the stovetop.

*That's okay*, I told her as the apartment filled with the smoke, *people become forgetful when they are happy or worried or thinking about the airplanes of soon and all you need to do is tell me which one you're doing.*

I already knew the answer, but back then I was the kind of person who sometimes asked people to say aloud what I already knew—it was obvious that Sylvia was thinking about the airplanes of soon and which one she'd be on and where it would go and what she might do when she got there.

I knew she'd do this from the first day she moved in, so it is true that I let myself break myself or maybe, rather, I let herself let myself break my self and by *self* I mean *heart* except I take issue with using that word that way, because I don't think we have any reason to pile such a responsibility on that organ, the word of that organ. Everyone knows a heart is just responsible for filling a thing with blood, except it never fills love with blood because no one can do that because love comes when it wants and it leaves when it wants and it gets on an airplane and goes wherever it wants and no one can ever ask love not to do that, because that is part of the risk of love, the worthwhile risk of it, that it will leave if it feels like leaving and that is the cost of it and it is worth it, worth it, worth it. This is the mantra of Sylvia and this is the way she is.


Sylvia found me at my own never-mind moment, back when the acupuncturist was the only person who would listen to me anymore. Doctors one, two, three, all said I was bluffing; doctor four said nothing, left me cold-toed in my paper gown. The acupuncturist wanted me to talk about my mother. How did I feel about her? Did she sing to me when I was a child?

Sylvia was the receptionist for the acupuncturist, but all she did was point to a sheet of paper that said *Sign Me*, and I would come in and she wouldn't look at me at all until one day she did look at me and when she looked at me, I also looked at me and I also looked at her and she also looked at herself and we both found we liked what we were looking at.

And so we found ourselves months later waking up in the same place all the time, going to sleep in the same place all the time, walking link-armed to the acupuncturist, the healing center.

But one day in my living room Sylvia stirred her teacup but there wasn't anything in it, so it just went *clank clank*, and then I knew, for some reason, we weren't going anywhere link-armed anymore.

*Do you ever get the feeling*, Sylvia asked, *that you're a lab rat?*

*That I'm a lab rat? That I'm a lab rat or that you're a lab rat? Which of us?*

Sylvia didn't say anything for a minute, kept stirring no tea in her teacup.

*Who is the lab rat?*

*Who indeed*, she said, and I said, *Fuck you, Sylvia, this isn't a fairy tale, Sylvia, you can't just say stupid things like that to real people.*

*I'll say it.*

*You won't*, I said, but she said, *I will, just watch me.*

# Learning

It's hard to know which of us began to wear our shoes in the apartment, but one of us did—one of us, then the other. First it was just in the kitchen, but soon there were tracks in the bedroom, bathroom, living room, everywhere. Old receipts and leaves crept in. The floor grew filthy. We got out-of-season colds. Ellen let clumps of her hair tumbleweed around, clogging the carpet, the drains, and I was no longer careful with the dishes, dropping plates and glasses so often we learned not to flinch at the smash, and though we still recycled, we did so poorly, never rinsing, never sorting, curbing them on the wrong night. We both knew the baking soda had been in the freezer a very long time, many years, a lifetime, but neither of us made a move to dispose of or replace it.

Perhaps, I thought, we had both given up together, both given up being good at exactly the same moment.

Around this time the commissions stopped coming and I decided to take a job I was grateful to have but hated to do: teaching (I use this word loosely) a watercolor elective at a law school downtown. Half the students came to class stoned or loudly eating take-out noodles from a Chinese restaurant across the street. The rest openly disparaged the idea of making something so useless as art, insisted this wasn't a *real* class, that it was just meant to be stress relief.

*Like adult coloring books*, one of them said, *none of this really matters.*

*And isn't that great*, I said, *isn't it just so great that nothing matters?*

They stared at me and blinked at the floor, or maybe it was the other way around. One yawned, making the one next to him yawn, then the one next to her, and the yawning spread like that, like a wave through sports fans.

Early in the semester, as I was demonstrating a technique for creating a nuanced palette, I noticed an inky bruise on my white shirt (we'd stopped sorting the laundry, letting the darks bleed on the lights), which would have been fine except it soiled my strategy of overdressing for class in order to be taken seriously. Friday afternoons already felt like the crumbling end of something, and it didn't help that I was just a mangy little adjunct in stained clothes with the perpetual look of having just been slapped. They blended their pigments into muddy grays and browns and fondled their telephones. They all had telephones and spent most of their time gazing at them. Some of them had two telephones; one of them carried, it seemed, three telephones.

How could I even call this teaching? All I did was speak to a roomful of people who made no reply. No discussion. No inquiries. Nothing even remotely Socratic. They were pointedly silent during the critiques. Once I tried to rally them with something like a motivational speech about how watercolor, unlike other water media, requires the artist to anticipate and influence the movements of liquid instead of trying to fight them.

*It's a lot like being a lawyer*, I said, shifting my weight from one leg to the other. *Or it might be like that. You know, leveraging a situation . . . The uncertainty and improvisation you might need . . . in . . .*

I returned my attention to the painting tacked unevenly to the corkboard.

*Okay, so who'd like to start the critique?*

Sean had disregarded the landscape assignment and instead painted a cartoon duck in a gray puddle. Someone sighed heavily, though when I turned to see who it was, they all appeared to have been sighing.

*Does anyone have something to say about Sean's landscape? Yes? No?* This silence, I thought, could choke a person.

*Okay, I'll start. So I think you're developing an interesting sense of line, but I'm curious, Sean, about how you came to the decision that this would count as a landscape?*

*It* is *a landscape.*

*It really just isn't, you see—*

*Actually, there is some land, right there—*

*This doesn't even matter,* Megan interrupted us both, something she had the right to do as the class's self-appointed leader. *We're going to be lawyers, not artists.*

Others nodded. Some were asleep.

*Well, when you're lawyers you can sue me for improving your graded-wash technique, but for now you're in my classroom and I require participation. Anyone else? Anything to say to Sean?*

I felt as if I were standing on a building ledge, a hard wind blowing in my face. Megan used a plastic stylus to make a note on some little device while cutting her eyes toward me.

*Well, if there's anything you need to say to Sean, I guess you can say it to him at some point between now and the rest of his life.*


When I came home from class that day, Ellen was crying, bent over her knees on the couch just sobbing and sobbing. I sat beside her and whispered, *What's wrong, what's wrong?* She kept on for some time and I thought, well, someone is probably dead and I must admit I hoped it was her mother. She'd had a long life, after all, and she was mean as hell and I never liked her, though I could stand Ellen's father, always chuckling in a corner and offering me Scotch again and again so he could freshen his own glass. In the last year her mother had become insistent about Sunday mass and Ellen had, rather quickly if you ask me, given in, first complaining on her way out of bed, but soon coming home with a superior glint, smug about enduring multiple punishments before noon on a weekend and all of this could be over, I thought, as Ellen wept, if only her mother was dead.

A half hour later she sat up, wiped her face, went to the kitchen, took a whole raw chicken from the fridge, and began rubbing it with dark spices. It seemed her mother would live another day. I watched her hands on the chicken, watched the spices darken its pale, dead skin, waiting for her to explain herself.

*How was class,* she said, staring out a window as her hands mushed the carcass.

After dinner we sat on the back porch and she lit a cigarette and told me she had been renting cars in the middle of the week, driving them in circles all day. North on one highway, south on another, west and east again. Her expression was guilty and defiant, as if admitting an affair she didn't regret.

*Renting cars?*

*Yes.*

*And just . . . driving around?*

*That's right.*

I would have asked more, but she made no room for it.

*Have you ever heard,* she said, then interrupted herself with a long pull from her cigarette (and when had she taken it up again?), *about that culture in ancient Mesopotamia that believed a man wasn't really a father unless a stone the size of his child's skull was shoved up his ass as the birth was taking place?*

She knows how much I love obscure history, but this blindsided me. She blew smoke over her right shoulder.

*My God*, I said into my hand.

She crushed the stub into a potted fern, covered her face, and began to silently heave. I thought she was crying again, but when I went to her—*What's wrong?*—she jolted.

*I'm kidding*, she said through laughter. *God, you're so—you're so—*

*I just take you at your word*, I said, remaining calm and speaking clearly.

*Relax*, she said.

*I am relaxed.* I was relaxed.

*You're so uptight.* She was turning the lighter over and over in one palm. *Sometimes I think it's because nothing bad has ever happened to you, so you can't even take the thought of something bad happening to anyone.*

*You know that's not true.*

*Name one traumatic thing that's happened to you.*

*This is ridiculous.*

*One thing*, she said. *Name one traumatic event.*

For a moment I tried to take her request seriously: I paged through the years—grade school, college, adulthood—and thought of my parents—kind and wealthy and alive and well, but it didn't seem right, it just didn't seem like a thing I should be doing, trying to legitimize myself this way. I stopped thinking. I crossed my legs and watched her flick the lighter on, smiling, swishing her fingers through the flames. Maybe *she* was the traumatic thing that had happened to me, I thought but didn't say.

Ellen went inside, made a big show of sliding the glass door behind her to keep the air-conditioning in—something I only had to ask her to do for about three years until she could be almost reliably counted on to do it—then she mushed her face against the glass, nostrils flared, cheeks puffed, showing all her teeth. A smear of face grease and spit was left behind. You only learn who you've married after it's too late, like one of those white mystery taffies you have to eat to find the flavor, and even then, it's just a guess.

And maybe there are times a person just tries to hold still, like your whole dumb life is a game of hide-and-seek and the seeker has just entered the room and you're curled under the coffee table and if you only hold your breath you'll survive another round. I was thinking of this the afternoon one of my watercolor lawyers, Leroy, seemed to have fallen into a trance at his easel after consuming a large container of hot-and-sour soup. He'd been still for a full hour. I'd been keeping a peripheral tab on him to ensure he was blinking, breathing, but the time had come, I thought, for an intervention.

*Are you okay?*

He stayed still for just long enough that I almost began to repeat myself, but he said: *I'm thinking . . . about what I . . . could . . . paint.*

*You know, you'd really be better off at least trying.*

The whole class had stopped whatever little work they were doing to stare at us.

*Heidegger said*, Leroy said, in a heavier voice, *that the possible ranks higher than the actual.*

*Well*, I said. My heart rate increased. *It's always been unclear to me what Heidegger's fucking problem was, but you'll need to get to work if you expect to get a passing grade. You can't improve unless you try.*

*We're not trying to improve*, Megan interrupted. *We have better things to do!*

*Everyone has better things to do*, I said to all of them. *That's not the point. The point is you'll never get anywhere if you don't accept that other people get to tell you how to behave. That's what a law is. What kind of lawyers do you plan to be if you can't even—*

*I'm just here for the attendance credit*, Megan said. A unified silence. I was nothing more than their enemy, I realized then. I stood in the way of everything they wanted. I almost cried or perhaps I did cry, though just a little. Didn't they understand? Didn't they feel moved at all by making something beautiful?

*Megan?* I called out, transfiguring my pain into anger, clenching my jaw. *Is Megan here?*

Megan snorted, folded her arms.

*Well, I guess Megan's been absent today,* I said.

Megan frowned, then smiled, and her smile slowly widened to show teeth. It was somehow clear we were both thinking of how her tuition paid my wages, perhaps only a dollar of it, but still. She was the customer—always right—so she carrot-ed that dollar above me, or perhaps had it there in pennies, flicking them at me one by one.

I let them go early, drew the blinds to the room, spread out facedown on the linoleum, maybe slept for a moment, maybe just licked the floor. I tried to hold still, to hold very still. It was not clear how long I would have to be here, hiding.

And maybe it was just autumn, that back-to-school feeling, that cyclical reminder that everything falls apart, or perhaps it was just the loneliness I'd felt since Ellen had become something more like a mean roommate than my wife, but lying there in the dim art studio I began to think back to college, specifically of that guy Jared—a townie, some years older, a sort of suspicious person but the right kind of suspicious for the time. We did Jägermeister shots, drove drunk, set an old couch on fire—or rather, he did all these things and I warmed my palms in the heat of his wildness. We spent whole weekends smoking terrible pot and listening to worse music. He had a vast collection of bootleg Grateful Dead cassettes and approximately one emotion.

After a few months Jared and I had a falling out and I wondered if perhaps this would have counted, to Ellen, as a traumatic event.

It was spring break and we were stoned at his apartment, which I later realized was just a motel room. We had been playing video games and drinking grape soda for a few days when there was a knock at the door. Jared went to open it and another Jared was there. Jared shook Jared's hand and the new Jared came in, sat down, took my controller, and started playing my side of *Mario Kart*. I was saying *What the fuck?* over and over, until I realized I actually hadn't been speaking at all, was just slumped over, stunned. Both Jareds looked at me. One of them asked the other if he thought I was okay. The asked Jared shrugged at the asking Jared. Eventually I found the energy to run out of there without my shoes, ran until I realized neither Jared was chasing me, that they had both just let me go. The next day when Jared came by my dorm I pretended not to be home, stared at the door until the knocking went away.

Weeks later I found him lurking outside the science building after my chemistry class. He had my shoes in a plastic grocery bag, said he owed me an apology. Turns out he had a twin, had planned this whole thing as a prank.

*You freaked out pretty bad, dude. I guess that bud's pretty strong or something*, I remember him saying, kicking at the ground, and another thing, he said, he had to come clean about—*come clean*, those were his actual words—was that he wasn't twenty-five, he was nineteen and a half with a good fake ID, and he hadn't really been homeless for a year, that really he just had a lying problem, though he was working on it.

How did one actually *work* on such a problem? And what do you even do with someone who tells you they have a lying problem? Could they be lying about their lying problem? And what was the difference, other than rhetoric, between a liar and a person with a lying problem? I imagined his lying problem as a calculus equation so large he would have no choice but to give up on it and live in that motel room forever.

*But I swear I'll pay you back, for the grand, I mean, and the plane
ticket.*

*It doesn't matter,* I said, because it didn't. My grandfather, who
had died when I was a baby, had set up a trust fund so large and
swelling it frightened me, so I'd just been giving away. Months
before, when Jared asked me for a thousand dollars and a round-trip
ticket to Milwaukee, I didn't even ask him why. I'd nearly forgotten
about it.

*It matters to me, dude,* Jared said. *It matters to me. I've been working on getting my shit together, on, like, growing up and shit.*

*It's really okay.* I walked back to my dorm and Jared biked his
little stunt bike in the other direction and I never saw him again. I
had decided just then that Jared's aesthetic didn't suit me anymore
and I was going to steer my life in some other, better way. I was
going to start tucking my shirt in. I was going to cut my hair.

But there on the art-studio floor, defeated, I felt oddly sentimental about Jared, how he wore shorts and Tevas year-round, how he
seemed to feel nothing. Before Ellen became my mean roommate,
long before she was even my wife, back when our talking was
50 percent backstory and no percent groceries, she would often tell
me of the litany of horrible things that had happened to her, each
time telling me the lesson she'd learned from the trauma, so maybe
Jared had taught me that if someone tells you his whole family was
killed in a house fire and he'd been surviving on his own since he
was sixteen and that person is also selling drugs you've never even
heard of, and if he's also living in a motel room and says everything
in the exact same tone of voice—maybe that is just too many things
and you should avoid that person. Still, I wondered what had become of him, his lying problem, his obscure drug business. Had he
gone to jail? Had he ever gotten his shit together? And how could
you even tell if a person has effectively gathered their shit?

I must admit, I find it both convenient and upsetting how easy

it is to find a person now, how you can just type a name into a telephone and more often, it seems, than not, you can find a trace of
them—a job, college, odd photograph, wedding announcement,
mug shot, obituary as survivor or subject. It seems anyone can seem
to know where almost anyone else seems to be.

Though I felt that Jared should be unfindable, a figment, he appeared immediately. He was running a highly trafficked blog called
*The Grateful Dad*. He'd cut off his dreadlocks, become Christian,
gained some weight, married, and created three small children with
an extremely pale woman. I found a picture of her on a post titled
"The Grateful Mom"—a low-angle shot, her pale hair and skin
nearly disappearing into a pale sky. I scrolled through the many
pages of the blog, went months and years back, scrolled through infinite comment threads, read paid product placements, the parent-
of-the-week series, the tips and hacks and softly religious prayerlike
paragraphs Jared posted each Monday.

I was still holding the phone close to my face when the door to
the art studio opened. It was Sean, backlit by the hall light. I was
lying flat on my stomach, head on its side, facing him.

*Forgot my hat.* He crossed the room, picked up a red baseball
cap, and hurried away.


That afternoon, I found Ellen in a fine mood. She was blasting a
Motown record and swaying around the living room with the vacuum cleaner. The smell of cookies baking.

I stood at the door and smiled at her. I was returning home, but
it felt more like she was returning from something, like she had been
hiding in a body that looked just like her body but wasn't her body
and now she'd come free of that other body and she was herself again,
uncomplicated, but when she saw me, the real Ellen vanished again.

*Home early,* she said.

*Isn't that nice?*

No response. She coiled up the vacuum cord like a roadie running late.

*I sent my terrible students away early, and I don't like to complain, but they are really just terrible.*

I told her about the Heidegger thing, and Megan, and their many telephones, and though I'd just said I didn't like to complain I realized then that I really did like to complain, a little. A little vitriol could make you feel human, give you the sense that you may be the kind of person who could break something on purpose, throw a plate at a wall just like that, just to prove a little human point. I made sure to leave gaps in my tirade for Ellen to interject, to affirm me, to say, *Yeah, yeah, fuck them and their laws*, but she remained silent, had turned the record off, sat still in the kitchen looking at her folded hands.

*And how was your day?* I asked.

She'd never been hesitant to tell me about her work, scientific research for a book she was writing on a topic that, to be honest, I never really understood. Something about tropical bat populations, or bat populations *of the* tropics (there was some difference in the terminology that I never correctly remembered, a forgetting that she believed indicated a disregard for her career—her *career*: she spoke of it as if it were a person dangling from a cliff's edge—so I learned to ask general questions). Regardless, she stayed quiet for a long time until she finally addressed her clasped hands: *I just think it's absurd that you think it's fine to complain to me about your job when you know you don't have to do it.*

*But I do have to do something with my time, I—*

*You could live on that trust the rest of your life—*

*Well, so could you.*

She scoffed. *You're going to go there? Really? You're really going to go there?*

*Well, no.* I certainly did not want to go there, and I had no intention of going there, but she, it seemed, was *already* there, so it was too late—

*It's not mine and I don't want it, you can keep your fucking money!* she screamed. *I've said this a thousand fucking times—it's poison. I've said this a million times—it's a complete sabotage to having an original thought to be that coddled—I don't want you to even mention the fucking trust fund—*

*You were actually the one that brought it up.*

Her face went slack. The smell of cookies burning.

When the front door slammed, a few hair wads and dust clumps were kicked up in the gust. I ran out to the stoop to see her driving away in a gray car I didn't recognize. She drove slowly, coming to a complete stop at the end of the block, signaling, turning left.

As night fell, I sat in the living room looking at that dent in the wall from years ago, where she had thrown a volume of *The Oxford English Dictionary* after I told her, a week after our courthouse wedding, about the fund, how much was in it, how I didn't really know what to do with it, how I didn't take anything out anymore unless I had a bad month or a client was late to pay.

*So you do those cartoon things because you—what? You just like doing it?*

I wanted to say—but didn't say—but *severely wanted* to say that it wasn't kind of her to reduce my hand-painted children's room murals to mere *cartoon things*. Instead I said nothing, though I could have said that early and consistent exposure to dynamic and well-crafted imagery tailored for a child helps to develop their understanding of space, color, and composition and is essential to their later ability to solve problems creatively. Or I could have told her that children who grew up sleeping by a hand-painted mural were

80 percent more likely than the average child to earn college scholarships and 40 percent less likely to behave violently or self-destructively as an adolescent, but I had told her all this before and could vaguely remember her disputing the statistics as *not purely causal*, but I suppose I expected, perhaps wrongly, for her to remember that at least *I* believed that my work had a measurably positive effect. Regardless, she was the one with the moral currency to spend, since she'd just learned of this kept secret and that I actually owned our apartment, had bought it in cash years ago, and there was no landlord named Alvin.

For a while I'd been making massive anonymous gifts to various charities, but the financial planner had rigged it so I'd probably never pay taxes again, which felt unfair, and later I found out that several of the charities I had donated to were shut down for corruption, hadn't done a fraction of the good they said they did—so I stopped thinking of the fund. When the quarterly statements came I hand-shredded them and flushed them down the toilet. I felt guilty for even feeling guilty and felt even worse for feeling guilt over guilt over all this privilege so I decided to do absolutely nothing, to just let it all sit there. It all felt unreal, a number in a computer somewhere that had been passed down to me like a genetic mutation.

But she wasn't angry that I'd been lying to her—she was angry I'd come clean, that she couldn't unsee this safety net below her.

*I could stop everything right now and it wouldn't matter. There's no urgency to anything I could make or do now—there's no, there's just no actual reason for me to, to even get up in the morning.*

She was pacing the room, her breathing shallow and hands clenched at her sides when she leaned over, picked up volume seven of the *OED*—a gift I'd given her last Christmas—and flung it across the room, making a dent in the drywall I'd done myself.

*I just married a goddamn university endowment!*

This made no sense but I didn't correct her. It was just one of those times when I had to let her say absurd things, a sort of emotional demolition. I understood what she meant when she said, back then and many times since then, that the fund was a curse. I just didn't think she needed to throw something to make this clear to me. This was the difference between us.

Hours later, long after dark, she came back from her drive. We went to the grocery store together, though we wandered alone, neither of us sure of what we wanted. I stood for a long time in the dairy aisle studying a $7.59 quart of yogurt after noticing an AS SEEN ON THE GRATEFUL DAD shelf talker below it. A cartoon version of Jared's head was on the container with a speech bubble: *The only yogurt I'll feed my kids!*

She and I reconvened at the register—she had an onion, bag of black beans, sack of flour, and Café Bustelo. I had potato chips and yogurt.

*Oooh, you got the Grateful Dad one*, the cashier said—*you got kids?*

Ellen said, *No*, and watched our groceries go down the conveyor. Though we used to buy organic whole-bean coffee from a local roaster, aware of the atrocious working conditions and environmental impact of conventional coffee production, we had, for some silent reason, switched back to the cheap stuff. We also stopped bringing our own bags, started saving twenty cents a pound on conventional over organic bananas, stopped obliging chatty cashiers with small talk. If they asked how our day was going we just stared at them. If they pressed further, asked us what we were doing today, we said nothing or sometimes, when we were feeling bold, we said, *Nothing*.

On the walk home Ellen said, *That yogurt was, like, eight dollars*, but all I did was make some kind of noise to let her know I had heard her, but had nothing more to say on the matter. We ate half the chips standing over the slant-ripped bag until I crumpled it up and threw it in the freezer to demonstrate our shame. She smiled at this; I claimed it as a victory, a sign that everything was really fine, would always be fine. A few minutes later I asked where she'd driven this afternoon, but hadn't noticed she'd fallen asleep on the couch.

Walking to school the next week I decided the real enemy of learning wasn't the students' apathy or their belief that there was no use in making useless things—the enemy was the telephone, how it made life seem to be happening elsewhere. *Life is here*, I imagined myself telling them. *Life is at the easel, noticing the world, interpreting it very slowly.* Perhaps I could turn this whole class around, make it feel exciting and fast, like an inspirational montage. It was possible that a few of them would abandon law school for the blistering uncertainty of the life of an artist.

I was passing by a liquor store and a small cardboard box advertising a vodka was out on the curb, the perfect size, I thought, to collect all their telephones on the way into class—no telephone, no attendance credit—and the first few students seemed at least willing to turn over their devices (though, yes, they were also a little reluctant, eyes narrowed, noses turned, ever so slightly, up) but it wasn't until Sean that there seemed to be a problem.

*Do you want to know what I really think of this?*
I didn't.

*You're taking a rather cowardly and immature stance to believe a smartphone has any legitimate power over the mind*, he said. *It's just standard liberal hand-wringing, pretending to be progressive and tolerant, but being afraid of every little change or advancement, and despising anyone who doesn't live in the way the liberals think is best.*

*That may be*, I said, *but you're still going to turn it in if you want an attendance credit, and technically, if you have one more absence I can fail you.*

*You're actually not within your legal rights as an adjunct elective instructor to demand we forfeit our personal property or risk failure.*

*I'm not a lawyer, but neither are you, and we both know that is a bunch of bullshit.*

Leroy sort of nodded at this as he came in, tossed in his telephone with what seemed like a kind of knowing happiness though he may have been stoned or already full of noodle soup.

I walked the long way home that day, through a warehouse district, then a rich young person's neighborhood that still believed itself to be a warehouse district. As I was cutting through a small crowd gathered outside a bookstore, I nearly knocked over one of those A-frame chalkboards. It said THE GRATEFUL DAD BOOK LAUNCH! 5PM! KIDS WELCOME! and someone had even re-created that cartoon version of Jared from the yogurt container, in flesh-toned chalk. The crowd was mostly women, ten to one, most of them yoked in one way or another to a child or baby. I was still squinting at the chalkboard when I heard my name.

*It's so good to see you!*

It was Anne, a client from a few years back, and she went in for a hug. I could not imagine it was as good to see me as she was making it seem. Her black-haired child stood below us, looking upset in that demonic way that beautiful children can be upset. I had painted a three-wall *Alice in Wonderland* mural in her nursery. It was based on the Carroll illustrations and had taken almost a month to complete.

Anne and I exchanged the kind of nonspeech that people with nothing to say to each other end up saying to each other and I even asked, *How's the mural?*—immediately regretting it, an inquiry about some walls in her house.

*Oh, we actually had to have it covered. Lena, well, she decided she couldn't handle it.*

I looked down at Lena, her little mouth pursed like an animal anus.

*I'm so sorry,* Anne said.

*Don't be. It's really not a big deal at all.*

*We really loved it though. It was just—it was really great for those few months before Lena started talking.*

I started to say something but Lena stamped my toe and ran into the bookstore. I pretended it hurt less than it did.

*Sorry, she's been weird lately, like, her whole life—she's just weird. But you know, like Jared says, we don't get to choose who our children are, we only choose what we teach them.*

*Is that what he says?*

*Aren't you—are you here for the book party? You have kids, right? I just figured with the mural thing—*

*Well, we thought we would, at some point, but I don't know.*

Anne squinted over my shoulder as if she were trying to recognize someone several blocks away. I mumbled something about how I was fine with it, completely fine with the way my life had gone, and just then I caught Jared's eyes through the bookstore window and saw that flicker of confused recognition, the wrong place for a person, the wrong person for a time, an awful reminder of how no matter how much your life changes, it doesn't. He smiled unhappily, broke away from the person he was talking to, and came outside.

*Long time, brother!*

Jared hugged me with that heterosexual back-clap. Anne looked at him as if he were a cake she wanted.

*Hi,* she said.

*Hi there,* he said. A certain kind of famous person just pretends like they sort of know everyone, I thought. *Can I borrow him for a second?* He didn't wait for Anne's reply before guiding me toward the edge of the sidewalk.

*So what's up, dude?*

*Oh, you know, man,* a nervous teen in me said, *just living, you know. And congratulations on all this. I saw you on a yogurt.*

*Yeah, pretty wild, but I can, like, feed my family and stuff now. Yeah.*

*Listen, is this about the money I still owe you? Because I had to settle a lot of debts and I'm really not liquid at the moment—man, you knew me at a weird time. I was such a fuckup back then, but you know, it's just that's how Christ had to teach me.*

*It's not the money, I don't need—*

*But I'm going to pay it back, you know, I haven't forgotten. I just— wait there, hold on—*

Jared dashed into the bookstore and I saw Anne watch him, almost go after him, look back at me, look at the bookstore again. He came running out smiling, aware of how everyone around him was watching him run, admiring his run, wishing to also run so gracefully. He was carrying a book.

*Here,* he said. *I even signed it.*

*Oh, you didn't have to do—*

*Yeah, but I really want you to have it. You have kids now, right?*

*Yeah, two. Joe and Chelsea.*

*Rad—so you'll totally understand this. It's part memoir, part cookbook, part parenting guide—you know, tips and tricks and stuff. And actually it's part devotional also, though marketing didn't want to emphasize that part—*

He opened the book in my hands to the middle.

*On every page there are these thoughts from me, you know, just something to think about—*and he pointed to a couple lines of boxed text.

*Jared's Thoughts: It's super incredible how all these great things can happen, yeah? Take a moment to think about all the great stuff in the world! #THINKABOUTIT #AWESOME*

There was a child's drawing of a bird and what looked like a fried egg beside it.

*One of my kids did those. And since there are exactly three hundred and sixty-five pages in the book, it also works like a yearly devotional. You know—Jesus really said that prayer can happen anytime, in any kind of voice, you know? Like it doesn't have to be all Thy and Thou and everything. And, you know, this was Jesus saying this.*

If there was anything I could have said to him then, I still don't know what it was.

*Anyway, they don't want me to push the Jesus stuff and I get it. I really do. The Christianity of old white men has to die, blah blah. I get it. And obviously, we're white men and we're not exactly young anymore, ha!*

I did not believe or did not want to believe there was a group to which Jared and I both belonged. I tried to hide this feeling from showing up on my face, just stammered something until a bright blue hybrid stopped beside me. I hadn't even heard it approach. Ellen leaned over from the driver's side to push open the passenger door.

*Get in*, she said.

*Curbside service*, Jared said, *very nice, dude! We'll be in touch, yeah? We'll get this all sorted out.* He shut the car door behind me.

*What are you doing in this neighborhood?*

*Driving*, she said, speeding through a yellow light. *What are you doing over here?*

*Taking the long way home—*

*And going to some kind of party?*

*A book thing.* I held the book up. *I sort of stumbled into it, but then it turns out I actually know the guy.*

*You know the Grateful Dad?*

*You've heard of him?*

*He's horrible. My mother sends me links to his blog all the time.*

We went silent. Any mention of her mother caused the air temperature to immediately drop. She is truly a wretched person. On this fact, we always agreed.

*You actually know the guy?*

*From college, yeah.*

*Weird.*

Several silent minutes later she stopped outside our building, found a spot right in front, though she kept the engine running and we both stayed in our seats.

*It's just—I think it's just—* She turned the engine off. *I think I just find it weird that you randomly went to this guy's book party, this guy of all people. This really isn't anywhere close to your walk home and it just seems to me— It seems to me that—*

She started the engine again and said, *You know how I feel about parenting.*

*Do I?*

It was something we'd never talked about, had pointedly been not talking about for years now.

*I've got to go somewhere,* she said.

*Where?*

*It doesn't matter.*

I didn't say anything else, didn't even want to, just got out of the car and she drove off. It seems to me you've got no option when a person tells you they've got to do something.


That Monday I got a phone call from the Dean, and that afternoon I went to his office, papers everywhere, like someone just aimed an industrial fan at his door.

*So we have something here of some concern, some concern, that is, to our students, the experience they're having in your classroom, and thus it's a concern to us, to the school, to what we stand for, that is, giving our students—who pay our salaries, you know—giving them the best learning experience we can give them. And I want to say that I appreciate you, appreciate your, your, painting, your, um, your enthusiasm for painting, but some concerns, some causes for concern have arisen and I just wanted to share with you some of the—I don't want to call them complaints, but they are complaints—some statements about a few aspects of your class that, uh, that bring them some displeasure. So I'll just read a few of these . . .*

He cleared his throat and began.

*"Instructor doesn't understand the meaning of an elective."*

*Well*, I said, *isn't it, by definition, something one elects to do—*

*"Instructor has something against lawyers. Instructor doesn't seem to respect law school. Instructor marks students absent to class when they are actually present. Instructor came to class reeking of alcohol."*

*Okay, well, you see, with that one, I found this box outside a liquor store but part of it, I later realized, had been soaked in maybe vodka? But I have a bad sense of smell and—*

*Sure, okay, and if you could just hold your defense until the end, that would be great. "Instructor drunkenly forced class to give our cell phones to him. Instructor openly wept in class. Instructor 'accidentally' drank and threw up a jar of paint water. Instructor seen sleeping in his classroom. Instructor seems to be going through some personal problems. Instructor is overbearing. Instructor curses too much."*

The Dean cleared his throat again, longer this time until it turned to a cough, then a hacking cough, then a truly worrying hacking cough. When he finally stopped he kept his eyes closed, hand on chest, peaceful like a corpse.

*You know,* I said after a long silence, *it's the pollen lately, or maybe the pollution, it makes my eyes water. They thought I was crying but it was allergies. It's really—*

*Listen,* the Dean said, his eyes still closed, *you're a creative person, an eccentric, and I really do think the world needs creative people, creativity and the arts in general, so I'm not saying the world doesn't need you, because it does, I think it really does, I just don't think it's reasonable to expect law students to go along with all your ideas about this, uh, this painting stuff. And honestly, the elective program was the previous dean's idea and I've been meaning to end it. They're lawyers, or they're going to be lawyers, that is, and we don't expect anything else of them, really. The world doesn't need its lawyers to be well-rounded. So what I'm going to do, because I am a reasonable person, is, I'm going to let you keep teaching the class, but I can't require the students to attend anymore.*

I felt like a map that had been refolded the wrong way. I wondered if I would still give demonstrations and set up still lifes and explain techniques to all the empty easels. I wondered if any of the students would still show up.

I thanked the Dean, though I did not feel thankful.

Standing outside the law school I got a telephone call from Ellen and I thought of how the story of this failure might entertain her, provide her some amusement. I had always wanted to be interesting to her. Perhaps that's how you know you still love someone, that their interest is still something you want, to hold their attention while they hold yours. It should be like two hands, like two notched logs.

She was weeping when I answered the telephone. I could hear her heave. When she eventually spoke she asked where I was, told me to stay right there, that she was coming to get me. Minutes later she drove up in a small red car. Her face was dry and pale.

We drove in silence, toward what I didn't know. For a while I thought maybe all her pain was over now, that maybe whatever it was had been fixed and we were really going somewhere together.

*My mother's in the hospital.* She said this as if she were telling me her mother was expecting us for lunch.

*Is something wrong?*

*Yes.*

*With her, or . . .*

*With her. It seems that, it seems—* *She's probably going to die.* Her voice shook.

*Oh,* I said, trying to measure how appropriate it was I felt nothing but relief.

I offered to drive but she refused.

*I love driving,* she said. *I love driving more than anything.*

When we got to the ER we stood in a long line, then there was some confusion over whom we needed to check in with, what floor or wing her mother was in. Finally a nurse walked us to an elevator, pushed us in, pressed a button, said to take a left on the third floor, then a right, then check in with the nurses' station there. Only after the elevator doors shut did I notice Ellen shivering and lightly sweating. I put my arm around her hunched shoulders.

*It's just that . . . It's just that she taught me so much,* she said, her tone a little more angry than sad.

It occurred to me that I didn't know what was (medically) wrong with her mother. I had been given no assurance that her mother's life was even legitimately endangered. It would have surprised no one if this woman had gone to the ER for something benign, then told everyone she was dying. She was the resident terrorist of the family, constantly sabotaging her own children and siblings and in-laws, setting off emotional suicide bombs at every chance. For years we'd been trying to get her to start drinking again because at least then she'd eventually fall asleep. She told us drinking was bad for her skin, bad for her waistline, bad for the glint in her eye, and she told me once that if she ever found an easy, secure way to have someone killed there would be a lot of funerals to attend all of a sudden, but perhaps, she said, putting her face a little closer to mine and lowering her voice to a whisper, *you wouldn't be around to attend them*—then she laughed but I couldn't tell what kind of laugh it was. When I told Ellen she laughed too, and we laughed together. (What kind of laugh, I still did not know.)

*She is a goddamn maniac,* Ellen said, but she was *family* and this meant something, to Ellen, that family, no matter how hostile, no matter how jokingly homicidal, was inextricable and *owed* something. It had always been a wonder that Ellen had survived a whole childhood under this woman's scorn. She had once saved three weeks' allowance for Mother's Day flowers but when the delivery came her mother took them to the garbage disposal and forced them down by the bunch. *They were ugly,* her mother said, *hideous.*

The smell of pollen now makes Ellen livid. Springtime is brutal. It may be impossible to unknow some things.

At times I'd wondered what, exactly, Ellen could have inherited from her mother. The only thing I was sure she'd gotten was a utilitarian bitterness that had always charmed me. She'd say things like *Mother's Day is just another way for a person to marvel at their own existence* or *The Freudian view of psychological development means parenting is a sort of fascism.* It was clear how she'd come to such conclusions and she believed them so fervently that I began to believe them too. When you spend enough time with someone, there's always this sort of balancing and rebalancing, like walking a slackline, a continuous correction. For instance, in the days after the incident at the hospital, we became even more absentminded at home, a laziness that culminated when one of us (we each believed it was our own fault) left a teakettle whistling in our empty kitchen, all afternoon. All the water steamed out and the metal burned and warped. The fumes seemed to be noxious, or so our neighbors said—they left voice mails that were at first polite, then increasingly incoherent. They became forgetful, drowsy, and after this, they were never quite the same.

# Touching People

She took them to see her husband's grave, why not, the newlywed couple, still sort of on their honeymoon, part of it, anyway. Honeymoons used to be drastic—plane tickets, passports, hotels—but now it seemed a road trip would do. It was all so casual. And maybe it should be, maybe everyone in the world could stand to be a little more casual about all these drastic things. Or maybe the newlyweds had it all wrong. Time would tell, or it wouldn't. Either way—she was taking them to see her husband's grave.

She had known the groom since he was a child, so she'd asked the groom's mother to ask the groom if he wouldn't mind stopping to see her on this road trip for a visit, so the mother had asked her son, who asked his new wife, who knew she wasn't really being asked.

Okay, so it was actually her ex-husband's grave. They had divorced several years before he caught and had quickly been ended by pancreatic cancer, but they had remained close despite the separation—that's how much they loved each other, that they could be divorced and still, you know, care.

Anyway the graveyard was a beautiful place, worth visiting even if you didn't know anyone in the dirt. You could see the whole town from there. And a mountain. Never figured out what mountain that is, but there, you can see it for yourself. It is certainly a mountain. Or maybe just a big hill.

Her ex-husband's gravestone had a trumpet and musical notes etched into it. They had always loved jazz, the two of them; it was one of their things, and she still loved it, but he wasn't anything about anything anymore.

*I can't believe how long he's been gone*, she said. *He was a good man. He was a very good man.* She thought his goodness made his goneness more tragic.

The newlywed couple stood near and the wife squeezed silent messages into her husband's hand, though he could not understand what she was trying to say, just wondered if perhaps she could please stop with the hand squeezing. She was trying to tell him that this was a waste of their life, that the hours this woman had taken from them were below the par of a walk through a forest or a drive along a mountain road or a ghost town or a nap. This couldn't be life. It couldn't be here.

The new husband gave the wife one of his Looks—his Please Stop Look. Basically they had gotten married because they could communicate, however unsuccessfully, in these Looks. She had a Let's Please Get Out of Here Look and he had a Just Please Be Patient Look and she had a Please Please Please Look and he had a Patience, Dear, Just a Little Patience Look. Anyway they had created a sloppy language of Looks and that seemed reason enough to get ceremonial about themselves.

The new wife felt the long afternoon they'd spent with this not-widow was not a reasonable reaction to the finitude of existence, or perhaps it wasn't that bad and she was just being tired and childish, a regression that slowed her sense of time. It seemed the not-widow might actually begin to cry, or perhaps she had even been trying to cry, but couldn't. But it was a beautiful day, the not-widow told herself, and she was here with these charmingly casual newlyweds.

There were enough reasons to live. She felt a surge of optimism, that all the family-court paperwork she'd filled out over the years had been worth it and she had turned out to be a decent person and had even become, it seemed, a little wise. Yes, she felt a little wise.

*You know,* the not-widow said, still looking at the grave, *I always thought of you as my son.*

The young wife wondered if the not-widow was talking to her dead ex-husband, or the spirit of him, or the idea of him, or whatever it is people talk to when they talk to gravestones. Had her husband felt all along like her son? The new wife looked up at her new husband and felt oddly maternal about him, though perhaps it was just the suggestion. But the not-widow wasn't talking to the gravestone.

*You really* are *a son to me.*

The not-widow rubbed the new husband's shoulder. The new wife watched. The new husband didn't know what to do with his hands. He smiled. She'd been telling him this since he was a child, to which his actual mother made her objection—*Every woman in town wishes she were your mother, but only one of them is*—but since the not-widow had a son of her own, same age as the groom, who had died, had drowned, at five, the actual mother thought it was charitable of her to let this old friend have certain privileges, an inflated sense of significance. And yet, the not-widow also made the actual mother uncomfortable, as she made many other townswomen uncomfortable, because the not-widow had always been hazardously beautiful and had remained so into her sixties—she hadn't had any work done, you could tell she hadn't. It was unreal. It was depressing.

The women who were unnerved by the not-widow also reminded each other that the not-widow never could keep a husband, never seemed satisfied with being a wife. Some thought losing a child must have bent her up in some permanent way, but others thought at a certain point (though all were uncertain about when and where this point might be) one had to buck up and decide to move on, not to dwell, to be mature, to blunt that old sadness, to leave it in the past. Oh well.

Another thing about the not-widow that made the townswomen nervous was how affectionate she was, how she lingered in hugs (especially, some said, with younger men) and always found reasons to touch people. What did she really mean by touching all these people? Why couldn't she just leave them be, leave them in their skin, leave them? Just that afternoon the not-widow had been picking bits of lint from the new husband's shirt, side-hugging him, fixing his hair, briefly holding his hand, and in the graveyard's parking lot when it seemed like their afternoon together was reaching a close (a "coffee date" that became "lunch" that became "a walk" that became "a drive" that became "a visit to a graveyard"), the not-widow put a hand to the face of the new husband and invited them to sit in her car "for a minute" so she could show them something. The new wife felt or hoped she was included in this invitation though the not-widow had only been speaking to the new husband.

The not-widow fed a CD into the stereo and some jazz began, then a woman's voice singing. The three of them listened for a while, the not-widow tapping on the steering wheel and mouthing along to the words. The song went on and ended. Another began. The not-widow offered no explanation but eventually she looked over at the new husband in the passenger seat, put a hand on his knee—*It's me*, she said. *I had been talking about it for years, you know. I finally made a record.*

The new wife, sitting in the backseat, looked at the not-widow's hand play an invisible piano on the new husband's knee. The not-widow sang along with herself, swayed with her eyes closed. Her not-son nodded his head, half-committed.

If someone, perhaps the graveyard's groundskeeper or a person in mourning, had joined these three in the car and asked them if they believed they had any choice in being whom they had all become, perhaps none of them would have said a word. There were just too many answers to this question. There were just too many ways of looking at it. Far away from the car several men were preparing to blow off the top of that hill or mountain, or whatever it was, and create a cavity in it for toxic waste. And farther away, deep in some woods where no one was talking or singing, there were creeks and caves that only the bears knew.

Anyone can visit a graveyard, no matter what they think, and every graveyard has been seen so many times there is nothing left in them for anyone to see and that is why we all must go and look, to see again what's been seen again, and that was why the not-widow took them there. She knew much more than they did. She knew much more and much less than she knew that she knew.

The not-widow delighted in listening to herself sing, in singing along with herself. It was a good recording, wasn't exactly great, though on certain listens it did sound great, but at least it always sounded good.

*You see,* she said, *everything can turn out beautifully. It really can.*

# The Four Immeasurables and Twenty New Immeasurables

### ONE

Last month I took an internet quiz about discerning emotion in human eyes—fifty sets of pupils, multiple choice. Now I can't look at anyone without a list queuing up—A. *Trusting*, B. *Hesitant*, C. *Happy*, or D. *Confused*—and even though E. *All of the Above* was never an option I'm still not convinced anyone could ever be that simple. One feeling at a time.

### TWO

The truth is I failed it; I failed that internet quiz.

### THREE

Another truth is, I know a monk who is trying to make the Middle Way go viral. He thinks *Four Truths So Noble You Won't Believe Your Eyes* could get some decent traffic, but he's not sure where to go from there. His other idea is something about the Eightfold Path or the Four Immeasurables but I'd stopped paying attention by then, distracted by his stoic, angular face in the late-autumn light and how his eyes never stopped darting. The wind tossed his hair like airborne snakes, those pale brown ones, harmless, found in gardens.

*Buddhism basically invented the modern concept of the list*, he said, and I will admit that lines like that—audacious and overstated—

have too great an effect on me, so unfortunately I might also be in love with him, in love with this monk.

### FOUR

The first thing men want to know if I mention being in love with a monk was whether he was bald, but the first thing Amelia asked about was his possible celibacy. When I told her he wasn't, she looked at me the same way those men did—disappointed, maybe, or hesitant or disbelieving or something. I couldn't tell, exactly, what was going on in all those heads behind all those eyes, but at least I could tell it was something.

### FIVE

I'm the only woman I know who swings hetero anymore. Most are either done with or never intended to deal with men, and I can certainly see their logic, but I keep getting these men in my life or they keep getting in there or I keep putting them there.

It feels unevolved. I feel like I've lost.

But what is it the Germans say? You can't jump over your own shadow?

### SIX

Or maybe just one German said this. One German. One time.

Or maybe all Germans say this, all the time. Maybe the entire German language is a slow discussion of shadows and the impossibility of jumping them. I couldn't say, wouldn't dare.

What I will say is that the way the monk gets worked up about consciousness and socio-spiritual evolution reminds me so much of the early days of the German, her theories about shadow selves, dark matter. Now I call the German by her name, Amelia, but when we met during her exchange year everyone called her the German. The German was known for her taut calves, hard opinions, and curls so tight they sprang if you pulled them. I am unable to resist this sort of firmness. These firm people. They are the shadow I can't jump. I find them or else they find me, mushy me, because if you're not making grand statements there's so much time left to listen.

**SEVEN**

A decade ago I was an intern at a media conglomerate, and the German was an intern at a different media conglomerate, and we spent most of our internships also interning for each other, auditioning for a possibility in ourselves. Winter was early and spring was late; we spent the long months between becoming the dust in my underheated apartment—greasing the linens, then cleaning them.

We were terribly young and naïve on top of that and sensitive to make it worse, but even so, it's embarrassing to remember how ordinary and lethal a heartbreak can be. (Feelings fall out of sync. Ideas stay ideas. That pebbly silence moves in.) The German was nearly arrested for jumping on a Chihuahua on Seventh Avenue, breaking its back, taking its life. *An accident,* she said, but it was just as hard for me to believe her as it was hard for me to believe how hard it was for me to believe her.

*Are you a vegan or what?* I asked one night and that's when we started breaking each other's things, a figurine, first, then the decent wineglasses, a banjo, an IKEA chair, a laptop dropped in a tub.

*Who have you become?* our friends asked us. I couldn't say, so I left town for as long as it took to turn into another person. It took a year and five months. My hair fell longer than a mop handle; Amelia's face grew thick and strange. Time dissolved us, those girls we'd been.

**EIGHT**
A. Wistful
B. Exuberant

C. Devious

D. Generally troubled about existence, human consciousness, the pervasiveness of suffering, and the fallacy of temporal reality

### NINE

When I told the monk about the internet quiz he actually laughed a little and that laughter lingered into a smile, and I was so relieved to see and hear him do something so simple that I'll sometimes spend an entire day trying to come up with ways to hear him laugh again.

### TEN

On a rooftop bar I watched a woman peering over the ledge, examining the distance between herself and nonexistence. I couldn't help but wonder if she might, through accident or intention, turn this place into a group trauma—if she might just *go*. Amelia came back, took a seat too close to me. She'd brought me a beer missing a sip so I filled my mouth and held it there till it went warm with me. What could be in a person?—whatever could be in a person?—I try not to ask myself this too much, but on rooftops I cannot help it.

### ELEVEN

History sits too close to us. You could explain the whole world that way.

### TWELVE

The woman moved away from the roof ledge. Her wide skirt swung and her face blushed bright. Here she was, still here. Amelia crooked an elbow around my neck.

*The monk went silent*, I said. *He took a vow.*

*That's your type, isn't it—moody and bald?*

*He's not bald. I told you that months ago.*

*Celibate?*

I shook my head, though I knew she already knew, and she shook her head in a way that wasn't discernibly approving or disapproving. This led to a debate about whether the desire for a man to ejaculate onto the body could be a form of population control built into one's proclivities.

*Why not take sperm out of it entirely?*

I thought she was suggesting we should—biologically, as a planet—remove sperm from ejaculate, like maybe that would solve everything. Maybe it would.

**THIRTEEN**

The first time the monk put a warm puddle on me, he said something dumb I can't forget.

*Your breasts*, he said, staring at them without attachment, propping me up in bed and resting back on his elbows so he could get a better look, *are my favorite kind of breast.*

There was something wrong about this. I couldn't decide exactly what.

B cups floated immaterially around my head—skin sacs of fat and nipple detached from their bodies—a type of breast, a kind of breast, breasts that fell ever so gently into their category of breast.

But categories implied quantities. Quantity implied supply. Supply implied rotation—first in, first out—how much of me did he even need stocked in his life? How dwindled was my supply? Did he get me wholesale? What was my retail value? It was a capitalist's fear.

If only I had a photograph of my eyes at this moment, maybe I could figure out what I felt about it.

I considered replying to the monk with a statement in kind, but no part of his body was my favorite version of that body part—except for his hair, thick and greasy. That, I loved. Though hair is less a body part than a cell graveyard, reshaped into an identity, a death halo.

### FOURTEEN

Another thing about the quiz: I could never discern *Aroused* from *Afraid*. Got zero of four.

### FIFTEEN

A few nights before the silence vow the monk told me we were isolated beings.

*A pure union is only possible with the infinite*, he said, *so trying to create a pure union with a human being, an isolated being, will just lead to suffering.*

He told me he was exploring the infinite through his body and this meant intimacy with isolated beings who were not isolated inside my being. He said something about attachment. He said this all so softly, while brushing my hair. I'd been sleeping most nights at his house by then and he bowed to me each morning and served me green tea in tiny porcelain cups.

*We must focus on the infinite—not suffering, not ourselves.*

I felt lonely and relieved, and I felt vindictive but peaceful, and still massively, terribly sad.

### SIXTEEN

Why do all my feelings come like street drugs, cut with something else?

### SEVENTEEN

While the monk was brushing my hair, my eyeballs were swelling wet, and even though he was behind me he somehow sensed that swell and said that tears are an expression of attachment and attachment to an isolated being leads to suffering. The crying sank back in. I didn't cry. I didn't even not-cry. I just sat there, feeling him brushing my hair, running his fingers over my scalp, kissing the tops of my ears, the back of my neck, the dull points of my shoulder blades—tenderness from a safe distance, tenderness without the eyes, tenderness between isolated beings.

### EIGHTEEN

The authors of the internet quiz used many different sets of eyes from many human heads, but there was one set, a woman's eyes with black liner and a little shadow, and every time those eyes came up I guessed she was happy, though she never was. Yet isn't it true that some emotions hide behind other emotions and other emotions are behind those emotions and there is so much, too much, at work in us, so much emotional spit-swapping, that I don't know how anyone can say anything about what anyone else might feel.

### NINETEEN

*You're not even a real monk*, I said, no longer sad, just angry, and when I heard him weep behind me I realized that's all my anger wanted, to pull something from him, so the anger left.

*I'm sorry. I didn't mean it. Of course you're a real monk.*

*You're imprisoned by illusion*, he said.

I turned to see that his eyes, in fact, were dry and easy.

*I've never called myself a monk. I never said that. I've merely spoken to you about the social evolution of the human species. Nationalism is the enemy of the collective salvation of human consciousness. Individuality is an insult to the infinite. How many times do I have to say we're all illusions?*

I wanted to know where that left us, as a couple, but I didn't have a precise answer to his question, so I said nothing. The truth is my memory has been going for so long, I don't think it will ever come back.

**TWENTY**

Like this: a stray memory of a bright summer morning, light splattered on a cat dreaming or dead on the sidewalk—why does that
wreck my day, my week, so completely? There's a word for the
scrambling of senses, but there's no way to explain how I'm always
reeling from unclear feelings and memories, no word that's not an
insult, anyway, or a diagnosis.

**TWENTY-ONE**

Amelia told me she'd been at a café that morning, and a man was
there with a baby, presumably his baby, a semitoddler, no hair yet,
just a wobbling grasp of walking. Dad was being real permissive—
letting the kid wander, crawl to the next table, toss saltshakers, get
dodged by waiters. After a while, the baby crawled under a table and
found something on the floor—Amelia wasn't sure what, exactly—
and being a baby, the baby put the discovery in his mouth and after
a moment the dad noticed the baby had gone silent and that the
baby had this look on his face like he'd just found a feeling he wanted
to unfind and the dad jumped out of his chair with a sudden urgency and he reached under the table and got the baby and tried to
get whatever it was out of the baby's mouth but it wasn't in the baby's
mouth anymore—it was, it seemed, deeper inside the baby. Perhaps
a little blood was also leaking from the baby's mouth, and the
baby's face was fading and the dad was trying not to panic, but the
dad was absolutely panicking when he shouted, *Is there a doctor in
here?* and his voice cracked like a teenager and Amelia said it made
her wonder what this dad, who was probably in his midthirties, what
this man would have been like as a teenager, if he could have ever
envisioned, back then, being a father to a baby with blood in his
mouth, eyes kind of rolling, skin going pale.

*Then what happened?* I asked.

*A lot of people stood around, then an ambulance came.*

*Was it okay?*
*I don't know.*
*Was it glass? Did the baby eat glass or have a seizure or something?*
*No one said.*

**TWENTY-TWO**

Because I don't know what happened to that baby, I can listen to Amelia tell this story again and again. Without an ending, it's as interesting as the beginning of a day.

**TWENTY-THREE**

The non-monk actually is bald now. He shaved his head, took a vow of silence, and went to a movie while it was still light out. I didn't know about any of this until he came over, letting himself in though I'd never given him a key. He has his ways of getting in; I'd like to know his secrets.

I said, *You look different.*

He ran a hand over his head and looked up, using his eyes to gesture.

*Not just that. It's something in your face.*

He took out a note card and pencil, wrote, *I just saw a cartoon, a kids' movie.*

Somehow he didn't have to explain the vow of silence. I understood this sort of thing might come with monk territory.

**TWENTY-FOUR**

But I also understood the difference in his face wasn't just the vow or the cartoon or his bare head. I didn't know exactly what it was, but I wanted to take it out of him, to prove I knew it was there.

I knew it was something very important and very close and very far away. Something as necessary and hidden as an internal organ.

# Small Differences

Whether or not I did the right thing—whether or not I was just being a "good friend"—whether or not I was lying when I said it was convenient for me to feed a cat for two weeks in an apartment a thirty-four-minute walk from my apartment—whether or not I genuinely wanted to be the sounding board for the serialized up-dates of his breakup (what she said or did not say, what he acci-dentally texted, what he can infer from her most recent tweet, Instagram, or Tumblr post)—whether or not I, to some degree, relish his suffering—whether or not he is, as she said, unable to care about anything that is not happening directly to him and whether or not I agree with her—whether or not his narcissism and/or solipsism is inextricable from his character—and whether or not my inclination toward his narcissistic and/or solipsistic company reveals something sad about me—and whether or not I even enjoy his company or have just become habituated to it— whether or not, in short, I am or he is or we are both terrible people, and how terrible we may or may not be—all of this is still debatable.

Nathan and I met as undeclared majors of the late, late twenti-eth century after he failed to be exempt from Intro to Creative Writ-ing. (The office-hour plea: *I've already been introduced*, a ratty stack of pages as his exhibit A.) His stories were the predictable homages in the style of an Important Male Novelist, often featuring a Russian exchange student named Nikolai: *The women is bad,* Nikolai said, *and we must not say so, but always remember, she is, all the she, is bad.* Nathan was commended for creating such a rich, opinionated character, but not by me. My notes on his submissions were all a variation on *Why should I care?* His notes on mine (gruesome crime fiction with unintended religious overtones) were usually arguments against my most recent notes for him. And I don't remember why or how because I no longer understand the state I was in back then (heartsick over the idea of Jesus the way that other girls were heartsick over the idea of River Phoenix) but somehow this was the beginning of Nathan and I sleeping together, episodically, for the next ten years plus.

I was the type to wander a Rite Aid alone and empty-handed, for hours—a favored pastime of a teenager wondering why a belief in Jesus no longer feels satisfactory. I stared at nail-polish removers and thought about how I'd never be a youth minister. I compared nutritional supplements while considering the conditional and imperfect nature of human-on-human love. Even attempting to imagine ever having a feeling at all comparable to the infallible devotion I'd had (or fabricated) with the Son of God was like searching for a needle in a haystack while suffering from a severe hay allergy and knowing, all the while, there is no needle.

A few weeks after I first met Nathan we were in a poorly lit park at dusk, and I was explaining how I got that lopsided-cross tattoo on one ankle and the shaky JC in a heart on the other, and I know it's trite to remember that he pushed a lock of hair behind my ear and grazed the backs of his fingers against my cheek, but that is what I remember happening so that must have been somehow important to me, and maybe that was the moment I accepted Nathan as someone who had a position in my life, a right to it, a tenure in it. And

I probably believed, back then, that he was actually *listening* to the story of my teenage recommitment to Christ, which had happened after lights-out during a youth-group retreat. Three girls from my cabin and I snuck out to the little chapel in the woods, where we all confessed to occasionally doubting the validity of the Bible and the existence of God and sipping from a water bottle of vodka at the Sophomore Spring Fling the previous April, and Sherry Evans even admitted to a blow job and we confessed those and other sins, together, aloud instead of in silent prayer, and we knew that Jesus would forgive and completely forget—at least, that was what the youth pastor had said, that if you were to ask Jesus what sin he most recently absolved from someone, Jesus, our Lord and Savior, would just look at you *dumb as a pancake* (that's how he'd said it), he'd look at you dumb as a pancake and say, *I don't remember.* And since this was what Jesus did, I knew that forgetting was something I should also strive for (*What would Jesus do?* was always the question) but I could never forget Sherry Evans saying she'd given someone a blow job (and who?). But then we gave each other tattoos with a sewing needle and india ink and some of us cried out of joy or pain and we all did that kind of praying where you have your arms out, palms up, face up, eyes closed, swaying, murmuring words or whisper-singing and I remember thinking about how I looked like a picture of a perfect Christian, like those people in the commercials for gospel-music CDs and I wondered if anyone in those commercials had ever given anyone a blow job but I immediately asked for forgiveness for having this thought, but had it again and asked forgiveness again.

When I told Nathan this story I was trying to cultivate an air of mystery to match his air of mystery and I probably believed he was so impressed by it that all he could say was *Wow* and start making out with me, but when I referenced the recommitment and tattoos some months later he sort of nodded and looked off and I knew he probably hadn't been paying attention, that he was just waiting for me to be done. Maybe I believed he had that kind of amnesia that Jesus had, that our present overshadowed whatever I may have been like before we met, but after Mom met Nathan on Parents' Day she said, quoting Paul, *Honey, bad company corrupts good morals*, and I knew what she meant but I told her she didn't know him like I did.

*I hope you're right. I sure hope you're right*, and I knew she meant, you know . . . Hell.

It is true that Nathan was "bad company" but that was what had made him good company to me—I needed bad company to keep the bad in me company. And despite several bad incidents during and after college from which it seemed Nathan and I would not recover (canceled plans and harsh words and his guitar thrown down a concrete stairwell), we did, somehow, always, recover. I once tried to rationalize that his name meant "giver," according to a baby-names book, and I believed that his inherent generosity would eventually become apparent, that he would grow into that name the way some kids have to grow into their ears or feet and I should just be patient. But then I realized that names are just given, not earned.

It's clear now that Nathan and I have always had just enough respect for each other to withstand a mutual disrespect.

I hadn't heard his voice over a phone in many years (we had changed from phone-call people to text/e-mail/comment people as the times had accordingly changed) so when he called that afternoon and said, *Nikky! What's going on?* I just said, *Nathan, what's wrong?* because I am not the kind of person who can tolerate these kinds of things.

*Oh, I'm fine*, he said, *just wondering if you could take care of Echo while I'm out of town for a couple weeks*.

I surprised myself when I said, *Sure, of course*, and he said,

*Really? You're sure?* because I've always had a habit of finding some extenuating circumstance to prohibit me from doing even the smallest of favors, but I said, *It's no problem—I'd love to*, and I knew I wouldn't really love to, and I knew it was out of character for me to be so giving, but lately I was wondering if there was a way out of my character and I figured this wasn't the worst place to start. We hadn't seen each other in several months, at least—maybe since that night at the Ethiopian restaurant when I told him I wasn't going to have sex with him anymore because I'd decided that a sex life was a waste, a liability, a bore.

*I don't want kids. I'm tired of boyfriends. There are other pleasures in life.*

He was either listening or making his *I'm listening* face. A single lentil clung to his lip.

*Do you want me to tell you what I think?*

I was surprised he'd asked for permission. The lentil was still there.

*No*, I said.

Actually there was another meeting after the Ethiopian dinner—a spring day in the park, a bottle of wine, a long talk that reminded me of those long talks in dorm rooms and quads that had cemented our friendship or courtship or whatever busted ship it was. He'd told me about how well things were going with Analiese and he seemed remarkably genuine about it, settled, not at all like the Nathan I'd always known. I asked myself something that I have been asking myself ever since: *Can people really change?*

*I haven't even slept with anyone else since I met her*, he said, *and I don't even want to.*

There's no way to say this nicely, but the truth was that Nathan and I would often have a little sex while one or both of us were in technically committed relationships with other people, but only a little sex and not for any good reason more than habit and it's hard to break habits, everyone has a few, and if it's just smoking you can smoke and say, *Oh, here I go with the smoking again, I know I shouldn't but I just do*, but if you have a low-grade, persistent infidelity habit there is no low-grade, persistent infidelity section in a restaurant or fifty feet from a government building and there is no patch for kicking your infidelity habit and there is almost no socially acceptable way to talk about being unable to stop yourself from having a little sex with a person who is not your Publicly Declared Sex Partner.

That day in the park, however, I was still on my celibacy kick, smug like a juice faster, and even though we later went to his apartment to watch a movie, we did exactly that and I fell asleep on his couch and he went to his room and I woke up in the middle of the night and let myself out. Since then, many months had passed with us saying nothing to the other aside from a texted quip, a like, a comment.

*You want to know the truth?* (This is Nathan, again, on the phone.) *Analiese broke up with me and, to be honest, I'm in a bad way. I really need to leave town.*

I'm mostly sure that a "good friend" should get no pleasure from hearing a "good friend" say he has been dumped and is in a bad way, but Nathan had always seemed so invincible to heartbreak, and baffled by the ones I'd been through—but still, I felt embarrassed by that small, reflexive smile that came when he said he was in a bad way and I tried to rationalize that smile by thinking I was just pleased to be the friend he called for emotional and feline support, that maybe our "friendship" was more than a shared tendency toward combat and a bit of detached sexual attraction. Maybe, somehow, we also had a real place in each other's life since he was trusting me with the life of his cat and plants, these lives he wanted to keep alive—but, no—I knew I wasn't his first call and he wouldn't have been mine. I can admit that I smiled because Nathan had finally been broken.

*It came out of nowhere.* He sounded like a televised local report-
ing a tornado. *Everything was perfect and then, just like that . . .
Boom.*

When I stopped by to get the keys I found him half-drunk and
glassy-eyed and chain-smoking though it was barely past noon. So
it had happened. He had cared more about someone than they could
care about him, and in a way I was seeing history being made, though
just the minor history of one man becoming more human.

*I'm sorry you're going through this,* I said. And the thing is, I was,
I think.

He said, *Well*—and he started to say something else but stopped.
His face was bending like he might actually cry, and I'd never seen
him cry except for that one time we took mushrooms but that
didn't really count, and he covered his eyes as if to turn them off
so I took this blind moment to smile, again, but that pleasure came
link-armed with guilt—guilt from being pleased by his pain, and
that guilt, that by-product of the Jesus years, grew stronger and I
know I cannot be held responsible for the guilt-pushed decisions
I sometimes make, because it complicates feelings, or makes me want
what I probably don't want or distracts me with what I should want
to do, or should at least want to want to do. This time the guilt
made me listen for the next several hours and two bottles of wine
as he ached over what had been so good, so perfect, and how could
she give it all up and what had he done wrong and why and why
and why.

For friends I can more easily call friends, people with a less complicated track record and a more obvious amount of empathy, I have
sometimes been that crying shoulder, that good listener, and it's true
I once considered a career in psychology or social work or some form
of clergy before I dropped out of college and stopped believing in
God—and I don't exactly read self-help books, but I almost do, and
I've undergone various kinds of therapy, so my vocabulary includes

*attachment styles, boundaries,* and *emotional dysregulation.* So this was
what I thought of while Nathan talked about whatever he was talking about, a sudden trip she took, a lie he believed, her saying he
was overreacting and him saying she was underreacting and something that he wished he could take back, something involving her
mother or his mother, a wrong number called—something, I don't
know—because I was distracted by the novelty of seeing Nathan
have such real expressions on his face, a rare vulnerability. He kept
saying *I'll be honest with you* and *Truthfully* and asking if he could
tell me something and then telling me something, but I was tracing our history back to the weeks just before I dropped out of
college, how Nathan had asked me to come home with him for
Thanksgiving that year and I'd said I couldn't, because it seemed
too serious, but later I wondered if I actually wanted that serious-
ness, or if he did. I couldn't get a good handle on it one way or the
other, but after a few days I said I'd changed my mind and I remember trying to smile a little more than usual, trying to be a nice
girl, trying to be one of those girls people take home for Thanksgiving, and he said, *Maybe bring a dessert?*—so I baked three pies
from scratch in the dorm kitchen, overly concerned with the lattice,
weaving and reweaving it until the butter melted and the dough
turned loose and gummy. He introduced me to family members as
his *good friend Nikky* but his aunt called me *the girlfriend* and his
mother just called me *Nikky,* always saying my name like I'd done
something wrong. Nathan and I slept in separate rooms the first
night and the same room the second night and the third night we
took the bus back to campus and he said, *See you around,* and
punched me in the arm and went back to his dorm alone. He didn't
call or leave a message or come over for two weeks, during which
my roommate kept saying, *Nikky and Nathan, Nikky and Nathan,*
and I said nothing until I snapped one night—*Do you have to be
such a fucking college roommate all the time?* She barely spoke to me

during exam week, then I moved out, dropped out, went back to St. Paul for Christmas and moved to the city alone.

The day before I left I called Nathan to tell him we needed to get a beer and he said *Sure!* as if it were nothing and I hated him and I wore my glasses and a sweatshirt and jeans that didn't really fit and he told me his thesis was going to be a literary novel and I said, *Sure, whatever, but what is this? What are we doing?* And he said, *What?* And I said, *My roommate keeps saying, "Nikky and Nathan, Nikky and Nathan,"* trying to make him explain who Nikky and Nathan were.

*Well, duh,* he said, *Nikky* (pointing at me) *and Nathan* (then himself).

*Never mind,* I said, and now I know better—no one should trust the feelings that occur at nineteen or twenty. Everyone should just sit very still until they reach the calmer waters of later-young-adulthood, that promised land of lowered expectations. Even so, I still don't get it—how so many people manage to keep asking the same person the same question every day—*Is this what you want? Am I still what you want?* without going insane.

*Can I tell you something?* he asked that afternoon as Echo rubbed her head against his knuckles. His face looked like a warped, worn-out version of his face ten years before and his apartment seemed like an expansion of his dorm room and our lives and everything in them a drawn-out weird-ass sequel to college, and I said, *Sure you can tell me something,* but I forgot whatever that something was. I was too tired to be good, to be tender, to care.

And then there was the cat. I was familiar with the cat. We had an understanding.

There had, however, been a series of altercations between Echo and me, years ago, while Nathan and I were in the middle of committing one of those low-grade, persistent infidelities: half-clothed and muscling against each other, we knocked over a stack of books near his bed, and Echo appeared, slashed my calf, hissed, bounded across the apartment, and later pounced on my back, howling, and whether she was trying to reclaim her territory or avenge me on behalf of his then girlfriend I do not know, but the next morning as I exited his bedroom, she was sitting in the center of the hallway, staring like a security guard. She made a low hiss, then waited on me while I was in the bathroom and when I opened the door she was all hisses and claws, forcing me to shut the door, trapping me inside.

But once she got her head stuck in an empty Kleenex box (or maybe Nathan put it on her) and as she spasmed around the apartment Nathan laughed and filmed the struggle with his phone. I said, or maybe just thought, *What is wrong with you?* as I took the box off Echo's head, and if a cat is able to express something like surprised gratitude, then this is what we experienced in our moment of eye contact before she bolted to the kitchen to hide between the refrigerator and the wall. After this she stopped barricading me in the bathroom and stared at me in a way that was notably lacking in hatred.

The first day I let myself into Nathan's to feed Echo, I could hear a neighbor speaking on the phone, a woman: *So can you figure this out for your own fucking self or do I have to do everything for you? . . . Well— . . . Well— . . . Well, if you would let me finish . . . Fucking hell.*

I lingered as I unlocked Nathan's door, trying to discern what the problem was, and as I put food and water out for Echo and felt a fern's dirt for dryness, I imagined someone else eavesdropping on the other half of this argument, also trying to discern what the problem was. I sat on the sofa with the vague impulse to read a magazine or take a nap, to make myself falsely at home, but I decided against it and as I left I heard that same neighbor say, *Well, that's what I told you*, all reluctant and tired.

When I came to feed Echo the next day I found the fern had been knocked over, dirt scattered over the rug and hardwood.

*We've come so far*, I said to Echo as she emerged from the bathroom, surprising myself with how quickly I'd turned into one of those people who speak to cats. *And now you have to go knocking over a fern.* She swayed into the kitchen and ate what I'd put out.

The vacuum was in the second closet I looked in, both of them packed with the kind of mess I remember Nathan living in—broken umbrellas, suitcases, old notebooks, coats wadded in corners, a dozen yellow highlighters and Ping-Pong balls rolling loose. It reminded me of his dorm room and his first apartment and the way this one had been before Analiese. Since then he'd lived in a sort of aesthetic calm: sofa reupholstered, shoes off at the door, art framed and hanging. He'd even repainted, correcting the smeared, patchy job he'd done when he'd first gotten this place and his first real job, at twenty-eight.

He believed his newly painted walls meant something about him:

*I'm in the no-more-bullshit part of my life*, he said.

I asked him, *Do you think people can really change?* but he didn't answer, just made us cocktails garnished with perfectly coiled lemon rinds. *I'm a man who owns a zester*, he said.

After the fern was righted and the vacuum thrown back into the closet, I wondered, again, whether I should make myself at home, fix a drink maybe, or read a book. I sat on the sofa and thought of how a former therapist had said that with every trauma, we create a clone of ourselves to do the "emotional deadlifting" and I couldn't tell if she meant your clones had to lift the "emotionally dead" or if your clone had to lift some sort of emotional barbell. Either way it sounded like a lot of work was expected of those clones, and I thought that my clones probably lacked the upper-body strength to do that lifting. I imagined all my clones sitting cross-legged on the floor of Nathan's apartment, waiting on something from me.

*I don't have anything for you,* I said to the idea of those clones.

Echo walked in, sat next to the sofa, and looked at where my little clone army would be, then went elsewhere. I found a book and started to read it, but I ended up just staring at the first sentence while wondering if I had a clone in me that had something to do with Nathan and maybe that's where the confusion of what to do in his apartment was coming from, the state of being close to him without actually being close to him, which, I was realizing, was more or less all the last ten years had been and though we called each other "one of my oldest friends," we weren't quite friends, just old.

My phone lit up: *Nathan Cell.*

*Are you busy?*

*Not really,* I said. It was nearing dusk.

*Because I think I need to talk. I need some advice,* he said, but he didn't really need advice; he just needed to be heard. I paced the apartment while he explained the situation, how he had defriended and blocked and unfollowed her and how that had prompted her to call him and what he had said and what she had said and so forth, but I stopped listening pretty quickly because I came across a shelf in his bedroom holding a vintage locket and a set of Russian dolls, both of which seemed to have some kind of sacred signifi-cance, and nearer to his bed I recognized a framed lithograph—and it took me a second to figure out why—it was one I'd made in college.

*And, you know, I get it. She's only twenty-five so she's scared of be-*
*ing so in love. Because what we had was fucking intense, you know?*
*And it's too much for her, which, you know, I understand. I'm usually*
*the one doing what she's doing, running—*

Yeah, I said, but he kept speaking without breaking stride. I
could have been on mute, I realized, and he wouldn't have known.
Then I looked at my phone and saw I had somehow muted myself, so I unmuted myself and said, Yeah, but I knew it didn't really
make a difference. I wondered how long the print had been hanging
so close to his bed. The last time I had seen it was in the old apartment and it was unframed and tacked up in a nook between the
kitchen and the bathroom, somewhere it could be ignored, take up
less space. All the designs I did now were on a computer, so something felt overly personal about him having one of my lithographs, a
real history of something my hands had done.

*How long has my print been hanging in the bedroom,* I asked, un-
characteristically interrupting him, a small jolt.

*Are you—are you at my place?*

Yeah.

He was quiet for a long second.

*I don't know. A few months, maybe. Analiese helped me rearrange.*
*I think she put it there,* and that got him on a rant about how much
he changed for her and how happy he was to change for her but she
never wanted to compromise anything—she just expected him to
come and go whenever she wanted so that's what he did and he
was happy to do it, actually—and he said something about how she
was closed to him or close to him and he said it a few times but
I couldn't tell which word was being said. *Closed. Close. Closed*... I
don't know.

When we were younger my attention for him came so easily and
I could listen to his endless opinions for hours and I suppose that
meant I loved him in a way that only nineteen-year-olds can love,

and though I don't exactly feel that way anymore I do feel some baffling and unexplainable grace, some exhausted affection, though he didn't deserve it any more than a jar of expired mustard deserves its spot in a refrigerator just by being there for so long without someone having the nerve to throw it away.

And I realized during one of these calls, which became a regular feature of my afternoons and evenings in his apartment, the phone hot on my ear, the battery chiming its impending death, that I almost never told him anything about myself. For instance, my father had died last year, a sudden hemorrhage, and I hadn't mentioned it. It had happened around the same time I began the celibacy thing and I had only told my closest friends because I dislike sympathy from strangers, even a postsneeze *Bless you*. And I guess this means Nathan really was more of a stranger than a "good friend," or a familiar stranger or a bad friend or some cross of both. Or maybe I was just trying and failing to do something like something that Jesus might do—forgive and completely forget.

*Hey, listen, I have to go*, I said, and he kept talking and I realized I'd hit mute again, so I unmuted and repeated myself.

*Right, of course. Hey, also, thanks for taking care of Echo. And for listening so much. It's been really good to reconnect with you.*

*It's fine. I hope you—that you feel better. Soon.*

*Talking to you is helping a lot.*

I wondered if I really was witnessing him change, if we were going to become sincerely friends, crying shoulders, laughing voices, people you tell about a parent's death.

As I unlocked the door later that week, the arguing woman was back—*You're going to ask me that right now? . . . I can't believe this . . .*

I pretended to struggle with the keys, a performance for no one, so I could listen in longer.

*You have some fucking nerve . . . When does your flight get in?*

I'd been spending increasingly more time at Nathan's apartment, bringing my laptop over, making coffee, ordering in. Echo would sit in my lap as I worked, as if she had forgotten everything that had ever happened between us. Maybe she had. Maybe I had too.

Most days during Nathan's regular call, I'd work on an image or e-mail. If I was feeling charitable, I'd paint my nails and mostly listen, maybe even try to find a moment where I could cut into his monologue, dispense some advice that would be almost entirely ignored. I started putting him on speaker and draping myself across the bed, his disembodied voice wafting around like a radio show trying to sound conversational.

I started thinking, abstractly, about inviting Zach over, this man I'd recently been uncelibate with, thinking it would be funny to sleep with someone else in Nathan's bed, but then I wondered if it said something pathetic about me, because I knew I'd be thinking of Nathan, at least a little, and then I would have to do laundry and I didn't know where the nearest Laundromat was, and then I'd have to tell Nathan I had done his laundry because I'd brought someone back to his apartment, so I decided not to invite Zach over, except that's not true, I actually did invite him over but he was busy.

*You're cat-sitting for how long?*

*Two weeks.*

*I didn't know you were one of those people who will be so accommodating,* Zach said.

*I'm not one of those people.*

*But you don't even really like cats. And you don't even really like him. This is the same guy with the Instagram feed that's all selfies, right?*

*That's the one.*

*He sounds insufferable.*

I knew Zach was right, that I had often suffered Nathan's company instead of enjoyed it, but some people are just drawn to other people and the reasons or rules behind whom you are drawn to have never been completely clear to me, though I've noticed I've often been drawn to people for whom I can set the bar of expectations exceptionally low, people who can never disappoint me because I believe they are capable of so little. Maybe this is another one of those by-products of having your heart broken by the idea of Jesus, of losing the belief in a deep and mutual love with a divine entity, and of realizing it was all a long talk to an empty cloud. I suppose that therapist was right and maybe a person has to make a clone to be able to handle it all and in the meantime a person can only attempt to search for another Jesus, someone who will listen—or seem to listen—and forget.

*But I get it now,* Nathan said over the phone, *what really makes you happy is loving other people. That's the only real point in life, and I know that in the past, maybe even with Analiese, I tried to protect myself from that, but I'm over it. I'm not that person anymore.*

I asked him, *Do you think people can really change?* and he was quiet for a little while and I could tell he was really considering it, and in his answer he brought up my religious past, telling me astoundingly accurate summaries of stories I thought he hadn't even been listening to, like my failure to make it onto the Team Jesus Cheer Squad and the time I'd stolen Communion crackers and juice and forced them upon neighborhood dogs and how I tacked up crayon portraits of Jesus in my room the way girls did with cutouts from *Teen Bop*. His voice was so tender and small, a fresh bird from an egg, and I felt moved by his little voice, or maybe just moved by his remembering things I was sure he'd forgotten or maybe just moved by the fact that I didn't need or want anyone to listen and

forget, that I was being comforted by Nathan remembering something that even I had nearly forgotten.

The conversation ended but I stayed where I was for a while,
nostalgic for the Team Jesus Cheer Squad. A lack of rhythm was
what killed the audition, as my stomps and claps jutted from the
other girls' uniform beat. Back then I was afraid this failure said
something about my true love for Jesus (or I was afraid about being afraid that this said something about my true love for Jesus)
and I was still lying on Nathan's bed thinking about this when the
fire alarm went off—a high-pitched beeping and a computerized
man's voice saying, *This is not a test. Please evacuate the building.
This is not a test.* But I gave myself a minute to believe this *was* a
test. I didn't want to get up, or stop thumbing over the past and
start dealing with the present. Then I thought I smelled smoke
and I knew that all you're supposed to do in moments like these is
just take care of your own bodily self and any nearby children or
animals, but that is not exactly what I did. I gathered all my work
materials and laptop before even remembering Echo and I tried to
find something to carry her in, but I couldn't find anything, and I
tried to pick her up but she was darting around the apartment,
rightly disturbed by the voice and deafening pitch and as I chased
Echo I could picture the cheerleaders lifting the WHAT—WOULD—
JESUS—DO? signs in perfect synchronicity, and only then did I
realize what an unfair question that was because Jesus had, if the
Bible is to be believed, supernatural powers, and his options—
walking on water, ripping apart dead fish to make more dead
fish—are not the options the rest of us have. All I could do was stuff
Echo into a reusable shopping bag and take my print off the wall,
which is also not what Jesus would have done, but it is what I did
because I am not the Son of God—I'm just a person doing what
I can.

On the sidewalk with a dozen others I was embarrassed about

how much I was carrying: my backpack and purse and this quite large print and a bag of squirming, hissing cat. A few people looked at me and I'm sure silently judged how I was being so materialistic at such a dire moment, and Echo began squirming with increased vigor, so much so that I nearly lost my grip on the print as she leapt from the bag and I was too concerned with safely holding my lithograph to stop Echo from sprinting down the street. I just stood in a dumb shock, and I knew that what I needed to do was leave everything on the sidewalk and go running after Echo, but I was worried about leaving my laptop unattended and I thought the framed print might get scratched or damaged and though I did make a small attempt to run after Echo, I couldn't exactly see where she had gone. Had I been thinking more clearly or being a better person, I would have realized my entire promise to Nathan was that I would keep Echo alive and in my possession, but then I saw the fire trucks coming and I imagined the soon-to-be spectacle of seeing Nathan's apartment building go up in flames, and that was more interesting to me than searching for Echo, which seemed hopeless and inconvenient. I thought she might not travel too far, come back when she was hungry, but then the fire trucks actually passed the building and kept going down the street. The alarm in the building stopped and a man with a ring of keys on his hip and a patch on his chest that said CLYDE came out, waving his hands like we had it all wrong.

*False alarm, people. Y'all can go back in.*

It was only then that I realized that I'd forgotten the keys. I asked Clyde if he could let me back in to 4B but he looked at me sideways.

*That's Mr. Nathan in 4B and I know his girl and she ain't you.*

*Actually, they broke up. I'm just cat-sitting. Except I lost the cat.*

*How'm I s'posed to know they split up, huh? I'm nobody's mama. I gotta do my job, lady. He didn't tell me to look out for no cat lady.*

*I'm not a cat lady—it's his cat.*

But Clyde was walking away and for some reason I held up the print as if he were still looking.

*See? I made this for him. We're old friends.*

It was then I either lost or found something, lost the part of me that was keeping it together, or found the clone that belonged to whatever Nathan had caused, and either way I knew I had not done the right thing—if there was a right thing—by choosing to protect my things instead of Echo. I looked at the print and became aware of its deep and undeniable hideousness, a still life with the bust of a woman pushed over, a pile of grapes beside her. How had this ever been important to anyone?

*I don't care what you made*, Clyde said. *I'm not letting you in nobody's apartment, lady.*

It was probably for the best.

*Echo?* I called a few times, but nothing came back, no cat, no assurance. I had a strong desire to be in Nathan's apartment again, to celibately drape myself across his bed, to hear him talking through that breakup, to be the shoulder he was crying on without actually crying. But I also wondered if I just wanted all this— to take care of his cat, to water his ferns, to pretend to be at home in his home—as a way to retroactively salve a hurt, a dislocation, a thing I could never get right, never figure out how to do. I'd always thought our history was just a history, but looking at that awful lithograph and not knowing where Echo was or how to get back inside, I understood that's the damn thing about the past. The things you do to people are always the things you did to people. My phone pinged but it was just junk mail, but then it lit up.

*Nathan—*

*Can I tell you something?*

# Family Physics

Y*ou've been going through a lot*, Sarah said on the phone.

Everyone kept saying this to me, that I had been *going through a lot*. I did not agree, yet I knew the "lot" to which she was making an inaccurate reference was how, in the last three months, I'd gotten married, filed for divorce, moved several times, quit my job, and driven to Montana, where I began working in a grocery store, stocking beans. Karen had called it The Blitz, though it's not like anyone died. But Karen is, by most accounts, my mother, so she has a certain perverted perspective on what I do, this thing that was once in her body, now walking around the world, messing things up.

*How are you doing?* Sarah asked. *Are you feeling all right?*

*I feel all right.*

*Do you?*

*Sure.*

*Okay . . . But do you really?*

*Tell me about you. How's law school?*

*It's med school and I'm fine. I'm just concerned about you. Dad said I should call.*

Ethan had called me daily for the past week, and before him it had been Linda, and before her, Karen, as if they'd organized shifts. It was hard not to feel as if I were a maybe-expired food that they were each smelling. I had always been the fermented vegetable of the family, but now it seemed to them (or it seemed to me that it seemed to them) that this rot had gotten the best of me. This time Sarah was calling to say she was going to come check in on me, for real, *physically*, despite my telling her I was fine, there was no need for a visit. She arrived the next day.

*It's just a lot*, she said on the drive from the airport. *It's a lot to go through.*

*You all keep saying that*, I said, missing a stoplight, horns blaring and tires squealing around us, *but what do you even mean?*

*Holy fucking fuck*, Sarah shouted, even though we'd made it through just fine. No one got hurt. She's always been nervous in cars.

*We're fine.* Then, after a long silence I suppose she meant as punishment I said, again, *Everyone's fine.*

I'd always tried to keep my distance from my parents and sisters, but they outnumbered me, were always closing in, always calling, always telling me that *family is important*, always talking among one another about what to do about me, and though I thought of cutting them out entirely, I had already learned the hard way, years ago, that such an extreme approach was more trouble than it was worth, like shaving your head—like any short haircut—some kinds of obliteration required constant upkeep—so I let my relationship with them get overgrown and ragged.

*Mom's so worried she can't even sleep.* Sarah stared into my peripheral as I drove.

*When are you going to get a place of your own?*

She kept staring. *I moved out seven years ago.*

*Seven?*

*Um, yeah.*

*How old are you again?*

*Guess.* She thumbed her phone as she waited.

This wasn't going to go well. I'd never been good at remembering things that meant little to nothing to me, especially years, periods of time, exact dates. I was older—I could remember that much—but I wasn't sure how much older and at the moment even my own age—thirtysomething . . . three or eight or six—wasn't entirely clear. Was Sarah old enough to have a habitual, though pointless, relationship with the newspaper's real estate section? How old is a person when they finish college? Had she skipped a year?

She interrupted my calculating with an eruption—*I'm twenty-fucking-five! You're thirty-five, Bridget, and I'm twenty-five. Ten years between us, and guess what? It's always been that way! I don't understand why you never can remember.*

She had wanted to insult me too, to call me a freak or a cold bitch or something, but I could hear her rein it back in. There was no reason for her to be angry, but I didn't say so. That's never what angry people want to hear.

*But how do you know Karen can't sleep if you don't live with her?*

*Because she's our mother so I actually talk to her like a normal person.*

It's true my family does many things known as *normal*. The density and hue of their front lawn can give one the feeling that imperialism really hasn't been so bad. My getting married had given them all the sense that I too might one day maintain such a lawn. It was all a huge misunderstanding, my being in this family.

*She calls me when she can't sleep*, Sarah said, sounding proud and put-upon, a vindictive maturity. *She's just worried about you. It's a lot for a person to go through.*

I could have told her there's no logical way to quantify experience, or I could have said there was no point in saying that what one person does or endures in any given week or month is, in any way, *more* than what another person does or endures, or I could have said that even if there was a way to quantify one's life, to assign weights and masses to the mess that fills a year or lifetime, who is to say that some larger quantity of mess was demonstrably worse or more difficult than some lesser quantity? Couldn't a life of too many small, pointless things, a life like a dripping faucet, be, in many ways, so much more terrible? But I kept quiet. There was just no point.

*Well, what about you?* I asked. *Aren't you going through a lot as well? With law school and—*

*Seriously? I'm in medical school—I just told you that.*

*Ah, sure. To be a psychiatrist, a podiatrist?*

*Pediatric oncology.*

*Anyway, doesn't Karen—*

*You mean our mother,* Sarah corrected.

*Call her whatever you want—doesn't she have enough to worry about on her own not to lose sleep over whatever I may or may not be doing? Isn't just being alive, just having to wake up every day, isn't that a lot to go through?*

It probably was my fault that I wasn't paying enough attention to the road to notice that older lady making her way with a cane along the crosswalk, but again, no one was hurt, and the lady may not have even noticed my bumper coming nearly within bumping range of her, though Sarah wouldn't stop going on, for the remainder of the drive, about how the woman had jolted, that we nearly scared her to death. I am not going to disagree with Sarah, on this point at least, that fear certainly does have the power to kill or nearly kill a person.

Some years ago, both wanting and not wanting to die, I made a series of decisions I now realize were not my finest decisions. It started when Karen and Ethan received a large envelope from my university—I had, they were all too delighted to learn, earned the school's annual Physics Award.

*You've never won anything before!* Karen said on the phone. If I had known it was going to be her, I would have never picked up. *This is marvelous. Just marvelous!*

I hadn't even realized there was such a thing as a Physics Award, nor that I was in danger of receiving it—though it *was* the only class in which I was doing well. Dr. Dabrowski wrote the words *very nice* several times in the margins of my tests and essays, and I had often looked up during class to find him staring at my legs, his eyes tracing them, unashamed.

*And there's going to be a ceremony in just a few weeks! It's all just so exciting. Why don't we all drive up to D.C. and have a little celebration dinner for you, how's that? Pick somewhere nice for us, won't you?*

*There's really no reason to do that. I'm not going to the ceremony.*

*Can't you just be happy for yourself, Bridget, just this once?*

I explained, yet again, that even enrolling in college had been a huge moral compromise I'd made for the sake of my parents—one last thing—but participating in this horrendous university's pageantry of meaningless citations and accolades was completely out of the question.

*This place does nothing but print propaganda about their alleged social-justice mission while they silence all the truly progressive initiatives on campus. Why would I want an award from them?*

But Karen didn't answer me, instead asked the familiar questions—*Why does everything have to be political with you?* And *Why won't you just accept that something good has happened?* And *Why can't you just do this one thing, just this one thing, for your family, for me and your father?*

(It has always been *just this one thing*, then another *one thing*. Like the annual Little Miss Portsmouth Pageant that all three of us were entered into at age six. For the talent segment, Sarah tap-danced and Linda sang, but I chose to recite a section of *The Lorax*, though when I actually took the stage I forgot (whether intentionally or not, I can't remember) to read the book *aloud*, so I just sat there, book in lap, face caked in pink blush and blue eye shadow, reading to myself. The audience nervously laughed, went quiet, laughed again, went quiet again. Sarah won it her year; Linda was a runner-up; I was nothing. Some years later at Cotillion—a series of weekend classes teaching fourteen-year-olds how to heterosexually waltz—I was sent home the first day for insisting that I learn the boys' part (not because I liked girls (I didn't like anybody) but because I didn't want anyone touching my waist and pulling me around). Cotillion was just training for future debutante balls (some colonial-flavored patriarchy dressed up as mere tradition) but by the time I got my invitation to be a Year 2000 City of Portsmouth debutante I was old enough to flatly refuse, though when Ethan and Karen found the ripped Debutante Society stationery in the kitchen trash, they spent a whole evening trying to convince me to accept it—*It's quite an honor*, Ethan said, *not every girl in town is chosen, you know*—to which I said I was well aware not every girl was chosen, since of course poor girls weren't chosen and neither were black girls or brown girls, and no one had asked Missy Elliott to be a fucking debutante and she was the only person worth a shit to ever come out of Portsmouth, to which Ethan said, *That big black lady with all the choice language?* to which I threw a half-finished Coke bottle at the wall. *I just cleaned in here*, Karen said to the sparkling brown liquid and glass shards. I went to my room and stayed there as much as possible for those last few months before college, wearing out my Missy Elliott discography, nearly blowing out my speakers. Karen would sometimes linger by my door saying, *I don't like this language*, while I mouthed the words to "She's a Bitch," on its fifth repeat. I loved that song.)

I remember this phone call with Karen about the Physics Award going on for hours, perhaps the longest we had ever spoken, during which she occasionally cried as I stifled my tears, clenched my jaw, and clawed my way through the somewhat nonviolent communication I'd learned to use in a workshop earlier that semester.

*Family is important*, she said, *and it's important that we stick together and support each other. That's what family is for.*

*But to value one person over another just because they're genetically related to you is really just an insidious form of racial and social oppression. I don't want someone to do things for me just because I'm related to them. That's not a legitimate reason to—*

*Listen, we just want to have a nice dinner for you. Not everything has to be so complicated. Should I put your father on the phone?*

She knew very well that Ethan and I hadn't spoken since Bush had been inaugurated, and I laid into her about hiding her own beliefs behind the beliefs of her husband, and if she really had, like she'd once told me, burned her bra in the seventies then why didn't she stick up for me last spring for refusing to be shown off like a prize pig at the fucking Debutante Ball? She nearly hung up then, but somehow we recovered and by the time the conversation ended we both thought we'd reached an understanding.

Weeks later, the day of the ceremony, I was still in bed when Karen barged into my dorm room.

*Today's your day! My little physician, it's your day!*

I was hungover both from a beer-pong tournament benefiting the Womyn's Resource Center, and a late-night screaming match I'd gotten into with one of my suitemates, Laurie, because she'd actually voted for that moron on the rationale that she was Catholic and he was *cute*. (She even had a W-of-the-month calendar, a dozen horrifying images, tacked up in her room.) Laurie shared a last name with a building on campus and happily called herself a *legacy*. She was everything that was wrong with everything.

*Are you ready for the ceremony?* Karen asked. I pulled the quilt over my head. *Your dad and sisters are waiting downstairs. I brought you a couple dresses to try.*

*I haven't worn a dress since Cotillion,* I said under the covers.

*But I think you'll like these—they're very plain, and they're school colors.*

I kept the quilt over my head, unable to shake this dream I'd had of W wandering the White House, looking for the bowling alley, eating a tuna melt off historic china, remotely blowing people up with the click of a button, and it was in this weakened state that I conceded to attend the ceremony, but I wasn't wearing a dress, and could she please get out of my room because I slept naked.

Karen left the dresses behind—*just in case you change your mind,* she said—but I just showered away the beer sweat and put on the same black Levi's I'd been wearing all year. First she didn't say anything about my clothes but at dinner she brought up how nice my suitemate Laurie had looked in her red shift dress. (All the honors students had gotten awards for being honors students, and it had taken nearly a half hour for all of their names to be read, for them to cross the stage one by one, surrounded by applause, and accept their little medals.)

*Laurie's a fucking maniac,* I told Karen, pouring myself another glass of wine.

*She seemed like a very nice girl this morning.*

*She's got Ann Coulter on speed dial,* I said, but this seemed to signal nothing to Karen, which frightened me too much to push.

*A toast,* Ethan said, *to my beautiful daughters!*

*May we all experience the right to make choices about our own bodies,* I said, clinking my glass to his.

*Yes,* my mother said, *there sure is a lot to celebrate, isn't there? Linda's getting married and Bridget turning out to be such a physician. And Sarah just told me she's going to be the cheer captain next year,*

Linda said as she twisted her engagement ring around, looking at it like it was the happy little end of her.

*How old are you?* I asked Sarah.

*I'm going to be ten in six and a half months.*

*It's the Junior-Junior Varsity Cheer Team*, Karen explained. *It's really quite competitive.*

*Start them early, that's good*, I said, but no one heard me. I leaned over to Sarah—*Men really do need a lot of encouragement. That entitlement's not going to just maintain itself, you know.*

She chewed a big mouthful of buttered bread and stared at me, then turned to Karen. *Mom, what's entitlement?*

*We'll talk later, dear.*

After dinner, Ethan decided it was a good time to deliver a speech about men, about how to tell *a good one* from *a bad one* (*There's lots of bad ones*, he said, *I hate to break it to you*), but Jarod was obviously a good one because a good man would have the *common decency* to ask permission before he proposed to another man's daughter, which is what Jarod did, and Ethan hoped Sarah and I could both find such *good* men for ourselves, because a happy life began with a happy marriage.

I was ripping up a piece of bread into little pieces when Ethan tried to cajole me, for some reason, by saying, *A good man is hard to find, am I right, Bridget?*

*What is that supposed to mean?*

*It's a Flannery O'Connor story. I thought you liked her.*

*Have you even read that story?*

*Bridget*, Karen said. *We've almost had such a nice time here, let's not—*

*Of course I've read it*, Ethan said, rolling his eyes and finishing half his ouzo in a sip.

*So do you want to talk about the part when the whole family is murdered or are you trying to say I'd be a good woman if I had someone here to shoot me every minute of my life? Maybe that line was supposed to be some kind of marital metaphor? Karen, what do you think?*

Ethan started to say something back, but Karen put a hand on his wrist like she was hitting PAUSE.

*Linda, why don't you tell us how wedding planning is going?* Karen asked. *Did you pick a florist?*

As Linda went on about hydrangeas I thought of midnineties Linda, the class president with a pierced nose and bleached hair, the one who chose an AIDS nonprofit for the annual benefit concert and didn't waver after getting death threats, the one with a pen pal in Olympia who sent her riot grrrl zines, the one who gave me condoms and Bikini Kill cassette tapes. And, sure, people always disappear into new people, and no one can stop the way new versions of people overtake the old versions of people, but something about the new Linda was so menacing that it made me suspicious of what she'd done with the old Linda.

*Can I ask you something? Why are you in such a hurry?*

Linda rolled her eyes but when they stilled I could see a little fear in them; she couldn't lie to me, not completely. We were all silent for a moment and I wished (not seriously, but I did (sort of) wish) I hadn't said anything to point out that she was only twenty-three and had abandoned her plan to do an MFA in vocal performance the minute that Jarod had proposed.

*Why do you have to be so horrible?* Linda finally asked.

*And remind me again—is the size of the diamond supposed to symbolize Jarod's cock or his salary? Or is it actually a to-scale replica of your clit? I can never remember—*

*Bridget!* Karen shouted.

*Are you a lesbian, is that it?* Linda asked. *Is that what this is all about?*

*What's a clit?* Sarah asked.

*I've got a tiramisu, a molten chocolate cake, and a spumoni, five spoons*, the waiter said to the silent table. Little Sarah replied for all of us—*Thank you . . . Thank you . . . Thank you*—each time another plate was set down.

I left the restaurant and no one stopped me and what happened next, I want to be clear, was not a cry for help. For years afterward Ethan and Karen were certain I was a suicide risk, and true, I did sort of feel like dying, but I didn't want to kill myself and I wasn't into drugs, so there was only one remaining option.

That night I called the girl from the Social Justice club whose apartment I was going to sublet for the summer and told her something had come up. The next morning I packed my few things into my Honda, and I felt deeply uncertain about what I was doing but also certain that whatever I was doing needed to be done. I drove west and kept driving west, feeling no compunction, no thrill, no romance of the road—though I can admit now it was a romantic thing, that I must have been at least a little thrilled by myself, that some compunction could have done me good, but isn't that always the problem—what we think is a moment of clarity we later find to have been clouded.

For the next fourteen months I committed no serious crimes, had no interaction with the police, drove as little as possible. I worked for cash, sold my things at flea markets, bartered for anything I could. I did myself no direct harm. I cried rarely, learned to use a gun. Occasionally I spoke at length to a person, but only if there was something to be said, something to hear. Usually I used fake names. I was never once at risk of falling in love or being seriously injured. I was almost something like happy.

And though I now realize how foolish this was, it never occurred to me that by not being in any kind of touch with any friend or relative, I would be declared a missing person and eventually presumed to be dead. That July day I returned to Portsmouth to get my passport I expected them to be angry at me for missing Linda's wedding, or that maybe Ethan would be upset I'd dropped out of college, but I did not expect my mother to make that strange little cry and fall over, to faint, to actually full-on faint when she saw me.

Their front door was unlocked so I'd let myself in, and though I could hear some people in the backyard, I'd stopped in the living room after noticing my senior-year school portrait on the mantel beside that obscene little trophy—the 2001 Physics Award. I picked it up—heavier than I remembered—then the back door opened, a wave of voices, scent of seared meats.

*Hello there?* Karen called out as I heard her heeled footsteps in the hall. *We're all in the backyard, come on—*

When she turned the corner and saw me she fell right over, almost immediately, half catching herself on the couch arm as she went down. I had never seen anyone faint except girls who faked it to get out of ballet practice—a real faint looks like death and likely feels like some kind of death too, because when Karen opened her eyes she didn't look as surprised by me as she had before, as if she'd long ago made up her mind that once she died she would see me again. What a thing to think.

I don't remember much else from that day. Lots of shouting, weeping. Ethan and Karen were hosting the neighborhood's Fourth of July barbecue, and when Ethan stood at the back door hollering into the crowd for Sarah and Linda to come inside, his voice cracked.

There was a question of whether the barbecue should go on, whether they should tell everyone that their middle daughter was back from the dead, whether it would have been good or bad news. It might spoil the mood, upset people, be too confusing. Some of the neighbors believed in the Resurrection, after all, and since the World Trade Center people had stopped whispering about the apocalypse and began to speak of it, plainly and loudly, whenever. They took me upstairs like I was something precious or dangerous. Karen and Ethan did that nonsensical happy-cry, a wet laughter, but Sarah cried in fear—the only person she'd ever known to die and here I was again, ruining the lesson. Like me, Linda didn't really weep, just got glassy-eyed and uncomfortable. I thought I sensed a sort of jealousy radiating from her, either that or she was weary from a midday beer wearing off.

*Linda*, Karen said, her face streaked with makeup, *go get . . . the baby—you've got a niece, my dear. You're an aunt!*

Linda came back with a baby on her hip, pink gingham jumper, matching bow, and the baby broke into a ballistic laughter at the sight of all these grown people crying.

*She's eight months today*, Linda said.

*She was a little early*, Karen said.

*No, she wasn't*, Linda said, glaring at Karen. *You can stop saying that. Everyone knew I was already pregnant.*

*What's her name?* I asked.

There was a long pause, like it was a struggle to remember.

*We named her Bridget*, Linda said, slow and hard.

Though I didn't want to, they begged me to stay a few days, but soon their joy had worn off and then came the questions. Where had I been and why had I gone and why hadn't I called and how had I earned a living and, really, what was wrong with me and how were they supposed to believe that I hadn't wanted to fake my own death and why didn't I care enough to just let them know I was alive and did I understand how expensive a private investigator was and could I even imagine how devastatingly sad my memorial ceremony was and did I plan to finish college and didn't I know there was nothing I could do without a degree these days and didn't I have any plans for the future at all?

Ethan kept saying I had *no right*, I had *no right*, and I knew that was the difference between us, that he believed that different kinds of people had different kinds of rights and that I, in particular, had never had and would never have the right to take my existence and place it beyond his reach. Eventually he and Karen began to talk about sending me somewhere and I knew I had to be going—not because I thought they could (I was mentally sound and not a minor)—but because this made it clear nothing was left between us to become clear.

I got in my car and began driving again, this American pastime—a boring solace or a bloody mess—though you never know which until it's over. I was in a Far West college town when I ran over a baby deer that had jumped out from between parked cars, and as I stood over the quietly spasming carcass, the days between leaving Virginia and being here felt like a misplaced set of keys or a fading dream—I'd just had them, then not—and I'd just begun to dimly cry as I watched this deer being taken from itself when a woman walked over from her yard, to say I shouldn't feel so bad. *There's thousands more of them*, she said. *It's just an animal. Happens all the time.* She took out a small knife and gently cut its throat, and the gutter accepted the blood as if it were rain.

The woman wiped her knife clean on her pant leg, folded and stowed it, and said, *Look.* We watched the deer turn dead. I thanked her for being there.

She smiled. *No sweat.*

I had this strong desire to tell her something, to tell this woman that her being there and saying what she'd said and doing what she'd done had changed everything in me forever because it was only then I realized I'd driven all the way out there—three or four days of steering—just to reach the point at which I could turn around and go back. I wanted to tell her of this feeling I've had all my life, but I couldn't find a way to describe it and I stood before her with my mouth open and drying out, waiting for a word, then I remembered or thought for the first time that when anyone tells a story they must leave most of it out, so I told the woman I'd been traveling a while, that I felt confused, that I was trying to become less confused but was only becoming more confused.

The woman wore thick overalls, a sort of mechanic's garb, a hammer hanging in the loop. Her face was all laugh lines and tan, hair like a wad of steel wool. And she said to me—because she had to say something—*Well, that's how it works, you know, working yourself into and out of situations. That's how it works.*

She was telling me her whole life story with all the details left out.

So here is what happened for the next few years, what happened with only almost all the details left out: I went back to school, got some degree, a job, bought a car, bought a house, bought other things, worked and drove and ate and worked and worked. I vanished into the map of how a life should go. I had a net worth and knew it. Karen or Ethan would call around the holidays to see if I was coming home (no) and around my birthday to see if I was alive (yes). Additional babies and children appeared in Linda's Christmas card. It seemed there was no limit to how many people she could create.

Ten years went like this. I cannot make sense of it. One day I was watching that deer die and driving through American prairies and plains, then I was thirty with a net worth and the same man sleeping beside me all the time.

Randall was pretty. I don't know where he came from. He combed his hair flat and cooked and cleaned. If I asked Randall what he thought about something he would say, *What do you think?* and listen carefully and often he would completely (or almost completely) agree with me. He had so few defining characteristics and habits that it was impossible that I was in danger of becoming anything like him. I remained myself.

Once I asked him if he thought it was a good idea or a bad idea to never talk to your parents or sisters if you didn't like talking to them and they didn't particularly seem to like talking to you.

*What do you think?* he asked me.

*I think it's fine. Or, I think that I think it's fine. It makes me sort of uncomfortable or guilty though I don't think it's rational to feel uncomfortable or guilty because I'm not doing anything actually wrong. It's more uncomfortable to call them than it is to not call them, and yet I still feel like I should call them. But I don't want to do anything just because it seems like what you should do, because a lot of the worst things people do they only do because they think it is the thing they should do. Doesn't it seem a lot of horrible things happen that way?*

*Hmm*, Randall said. Sometimes he just made serious listening noises like this.

*But I guess sometimes I wonder what they look like now or act like now, that maybe they've changed in ways I couldn't have anticipated. If you were me, would you want to go visit them maybe?*

And that's how we ended up back in that living room I hadn't seen since I'd been a just-resurrected person. The Physics Award was still on the mantel.

*It reminds us of that time we thought she was dead*, Sarah said to Randall as he studied it.

*Ha-ha*, Randall said.

*No, seriously. She never told you?*

*She never did. You could have been a physicist. Imagine that.*

Sarah resisted the impulse she seemed to have to tell him about that year, and he didn't ask me about it, then Karen was shouting to us about dinner being ready.

After dessert Ethan invited Randall out to the porch for a Scotch while Karen cleaned the kitchen and Linda's many children ran around the house playing a game they called Dead, in which one child would hide somewhere while the others announced that child to be dead, until the dead child came back and they would run laps around the house together screaming, *I'm not dead! I'm not dead!*

When one of the kids dashed in from the porch, I overheard Randall asking Ethan, *What do you think?* in that same tone and cadence he used with me.

Linda kept telling me I looked skinny—*Why are you so skinny? When did you get so skinny?*—but we had always been and were still, more or less, the same physical size. She just wanted to remind me, in any way she could, that between the two of us, she was the larger person.

And in the interest of leaving out all the details I will say that it was shortly after this Randall asked me if he could ask my father if he could ask me to marry him and I said that was fine, and my father said that was fine, and when I was asked again I too said it was fine. And it was fine. Eventually we were married and that went fine and we were a fine pair of newlyweds and people called us newlyweds with such a glee that I never knew where to look.

It was shortly after all this that I woke beside Randall to find Randall was already awake, sheet to his chest, hands folded under his chin. He was staring at the ceiling.

*What are you thinking about?* I must have been in some kind of panic since I rarely, if ever, asked anyone that question.

*The ceiling,* he said.

These were also the days I regularly imagined checking myself into a psych ward, a thought I had with the ritual and frequency that other people take multivitamins. It seemed to keep me healthy, this psych-ward ideation, though it would have been difficult to prove it had any effect on my health at all. I confessed my psych-ward-ideation-multivitamin to Randall as he stared at the ceiling that morning, and he made his serious listening noises and kept staring at the ceiling. I began to cry (who knows why, they came on like nosebleeds) and Randall's phone buzzed. He picked it up; an AMBER Alert.

*Have you seen this child?* he asked, holding the screen out to show me a little boy with small eyes and big teeth. He brought the phone back to his face and began checking sports scores while I soaked my pillow with silent weeping.

So that's how The Blitz began, as Karen called it. I drove to Montana partially because I could remember being content when I'd traveled there as a younger woman and partially because I thought I remembered someone mentioning their divorce laws were so easy that all the documents were written in Comic Sans.

*You are a cruel woman,* Karen said on speakerphone as I was driving through the Badlands. *Really, you're heartless.*

*Not really.*

*Well, you're doing a cruel thing to a good man.*

*He won't mind.*

*Oh, is that right?*

*He hasn't minded anything so far.*

A few weeks later in Montana, I was saying more or less the same sentences to Sarah as I drove her back to my new home, that musty old cabin on the deadest end of a dead end.

*No offense,* Sarah said as dusk fell, *but this place is creepy.*

It *was* creepy, but it was also the only furnished place I could find, and I wasn't sure how long I'd stay in Montana, just as I hadn't been sure whether to stay with Randall for another two weeks or the rest of my life, and just as I hadn't been sure, when leaving Randall, whether I should keep living in that house and have him move out, or whether I should find another house nearby to live in alone, or whether I should leave that city completely—and it was during this indecision that I began moving from home to home, all of them prefurnished, short-term rentals, trying on this kind of life, that kind of life, waiting either to find the right kind of life or waiting to stop believing there was a right life and just settle on one. During those nomadic months I realized I had no pressing reason to keep or quit the job I'd long had. There was often no reason to get out of bed, though there was also no reason to stay in bed, and there was never a reason to eat but never a reason to starve. Reasons were in short supply. Whether to smoke or not smoke—no reason—and when given the choice to speak or not speak I found no reason to do either and when I looked back at past choices I couldn't identify a reason for any of them—no reason to marry Randall, to own a car, to have a job, to live in one city or another, one state or another, to finally go to that long-imagined psych ward or find some other end to live in—and now, reasonless in a red state, the possibilities were infinite and nonexistent.

All of which is to say, I was the ideal person to rent a creepy little cabin someone had just tidied up after their batty grandfather finally died in his sleep.

*Isn't there anywhere we could go tonight*, Sarah asked, *something we could do?*

Coincidentally, a party was happening that night, though I'd already planned to not attend. Not because I didn't like parties—I did, sort of—and not because Sarah had arrived that day, but because I didn't feel I had been invited. I *had* been invited (technically) just as everyone else who worked at the grocery store had been invited. It was the annual storewide bonfire; they'd even moved closing time up an hour and a half so everyone could make it.

She and I took shots of bourbon before leaving the cabin, preparing to get drunk enough to feel or at least behave sisterly. Sarah, for many reasons, had always seemed like someone else's sister, and when I had to refer to her as *my sister Sarah*, I felt fraudulent, even a little perverted. Bourbon was a temporary fix for this.

By the time we arrived the bonfire was already going. The cashier with the horse face was playing the fiddle off to the side of the group, as if she'd been hired to do so. A few guys from the cheese department were huddled together sharing a joint and my supervisor, Betty, was holding someone's leg as they did a keg stand.

*What's your department again?* one of the stoned cheese guys asked.

*Beans*, I said. He frowned, tilted his face. *I mean bulk. It's just all beans to me.*

The cheese guy was still laughing at this and I was still silent when Sarah brought me a second beer, a local ale that tasted like it was from nowhere in particular.

*What's so funny?* she asked.

*Beans*, I said.

*What?*

The cheese guy laughed even louder, but gathered himself to ask Sarah, *What's* your *department?*

*I'm her sister.* She nudged me.

*Ah, cool, cool. Family department, cool.*

*No, I'm just visiting*, Sarah said, defensive in at least three ways.

Just then the cashier who looked for numerological significance in her customers' totals came up and hugged me.

*Bridget, I am so glad you're here.* She hugged me again, harder this time and rocking us side to side. My arms dangled. Sarah stared.

*Your total from yesterday—eight dollars and eighty-eight cents—I looked it up and it's a very lucky number in the Chinese tradition. It means wealthy wealthy wealthy—isn't that great news?*

The items that had brought me to this total were some olives, a tiny wedge of expensive cheese, and a box of cereal. Groceries of the lonely. The cashier's excitement over the meaning behind the total—*My first triple all month!*—only increased my feeling of total reasonlessness.

*She's wealthy already*, Sarah said, only half-drunk but already childish, already sisterly. *She's totally loaded.*

The cheese guy and cashier both turned to Sarah and Sarah looked to me, looked for one of those wordless reproaches that run in our family, but I had nothing, no expression at all.

*She's right. I don't even need a job. I have no reason to be here.*

Disbelieving, the cheese guy high-fived me, chuckled, and went off toward the keg.

The cashier began reading Sarah's aura. *I can see you're in a transitional phase.*

*Aren't we all?* Sarah replied.

*You know, you are so right. It's a very strange time in this country, isn't it? Very transitional.*

I sensed they were about to talk politics, the election just over, everyone doing that same dejected head-shaking. A series of graffiti that had appeared on a nearby bridge spared no race, gender, or political affiliation. *Fuck everything.* Someone had even scrawled *Fuck Abolition,* though maybe it said *Abortion,* but wasn't that all part of the problem, the words, the facts? The million details left out?

I lowered my empty Solo cup to see Sarah lying on a tarp nearby, the cashier administering what looked like Reiki. A few others sat cross-legged, watching, smiling.

At the keg I listened to that woman from HR as she twirled the gray end of her side braid.

*My daughter—she's sixteen—and all her friends at school, well, they're all upset, real upset about it and they decided to organize a peace ceremony. Isn't that nice?*

The man refilling his beer nodded—*Real nice,* he said—and handed me the tap.

The party went on. The keg got tapped and out came the whiskeys. One of the cheese guys asked Sarah for her number and didn't seem to understand what she meant when she told him, several times, that she was *just visiting.*

*We need to go*, she said, leaning into me. *Are those cheese boys always so handsy?*

On the walk home we locked arms, the alcohol bringing us together, as intended. Sarah's phone buzzed and it was Linda—she'd found a cheap overnight flight and was on her way out too.

*Is this some sort of intervention?*

*Noooo, nuh-uh.* Sarah shook her head in a way that reminded me of when she was a baby, shaking her head at almost everything— applesauce, car seats, the television. Once a discontent, then a cheerleader.

*It's a sisters weekend is what it is!* Sarah shouted. *It's fun!*

*But . . . why? We aren't those sort of sisters.*

*Actually, I do have something to tell you.* We were just outside my creepy little cabin, the porch light flickering. *I'm engaged!*

I was still waiting for her to tell me something until I realized that was it. *Oh! Congratulations. To whom?*

She turned her phone screen to me, bleaching my night vision. It was a picture of Sarah and a gray-haired man, their faces pressed together at the cheek.

*Wait—is that Mr. Jacobsen? From . . . wasn't he?*

*His name's Charlie and, yes, he's Claire-Anne's stepdad, well, her ex-stepdad.*

*Isn't he . . . is he Dad's age?*

*He's only forty-eight.*

I started to say something but caught myself, began again, caught myself again. I went inside and she followed. I poured us large cups of bourbon.

*You know, my twenty-five isn't the same as your twenty-five and you don't have to be so moralizing about it, you know—I just, I wanted to tell you in person.* I handed her the bourbon. *Thank you. Doesn't that mean anything to you? Me coming all the way out here just to tell you?*

*Yes. That means something . . . and I am happy for you, if you're happy for you. It's just I'm not that happy of a person.*

As I said this I sat on the defective reclining chair, which jerked me backward; my bourbon splashed across my face. If we had been a different sort of sisters, maybe this would have been the comic relief to the night, the laughing end to our troubles, but Sarah just threw me a dishrag and poured half her drink into my empty cup. The rest of the night was a smear. Soon we were asleep.

The next morning, quite early, Linda was there, and though I didn't know what time it was, I knew it was too early for anyone to open anyone's front door shouting, *Helloooo!* But nothing can stop Linda and nothing has ever stopped Linda from doing what she thinks she wants to do. Sarah was still facedown on her pallet, moaning, when I came downstairs to find Linda rolling her luggage in from a rental car parked out front.

*You must be tired,* I told her, *you can take my bed if—*

*Bridget, I have five kids—*

*Is that all?*

*An overnight flight alone, even with two layovers, is a vacation in itself. Did Sarah tell you the good news?*

*I told her,* Sarah said, half-muffled by the pillow, eyes still shut.

*Isn't it so great? And how are you?* Linda shouted after me as I headed toward the galley kitchen. *You sure have been going through a lot.*

*Well, it's not like I have five kids.*

*And what's that supposed to mean?*

I said nothing to this, just leaned over and drank straight from the faucet.

*Never mind*, Linda said, *I'm just being cranky, I barely slept.*

*Sleep. Everyone, go back to sleep*, Sarah said like a child from the floor.

*What did you guys do last night?*

*Sarah met a new suitor and learned some satanic rituals*, I said.

*Is that so?* Linda looked down at Sarah.

*Please go away, sleep now, bye-bye*, Sarah said, so I took Linda to a twenty-four-hour diner I liked because the food and service were so terrible it took me hours to order or consume anything there. I'd always felt at home in that greasy air, but now that Linda was with me I felt unnatural. We didn't know how to be around each other, casually like this, drinking coffee, passing the time.

*Don't you sort of think that forty-eight is just too old?*

*Oh, but Sarah is very mature*, Linda said.

*But she still sleeps with that blanket. She even travels with it.*

*That's more like a tradition. It's just a little rag at this point.*

*She's twenty-five.*

*You know, her twenty-five isn't the same as your twenty-five.*

*Oh, believe me, I know.*

*Anyway, she's an adult. I really don't see anything wrong with it.*

*Here you go, gals*, the waitress said, setting a cold disk of hash browns between us. Linda immediately blotted it with paper napkins and began to cut it into bite-size pieces.

*Oh my God, sorry*, she said. *You know, I did this a few weeks ago to my own steak while Jarod and I were supposed to be on a date. We had driven all the way to the coast for a nice dinner and I was still . . . you know, on automatic.*

Linda set the cutlery down, put her hands in her lap.

*To be honest—and I didn't think it was all right to tell Sarah this right now, since everything is going so well for her—but I can tell you, at least, that Jarod and I, well, things are just—Jarod has, um . . . We're trying to work through, we've been trying to work through some . . .*

*issues but we maybe think, we might, things might be better if we . . .*
*You know. If we . . .*

I thought I was good at crying discreetly in public, but that morning Linda made me realize that a public cry was truly an art that contained possibilities I hadn't previously known. She didn't heave, didn't scrunch her face, was completely silent. Her cheeks just flushed pink and the tears funneled straight down her face and into her coffee cup as she sipped. I had never felt so related to her.

*Well, enough about that,* she said. *When was the last time you saw the kids?*

She already had her phone out, was scrolling through photos—here they were at the beach, at a Fourth of July parade, Easter Sunday, a school play. And here was Bebe—that's what they'd started calling Bridget once I wasn't dead anymore—before her Cotillion. Here was Oak's first day at preschool. William in his T-ball uniform. Jarod Jr. and Jessica playing dolls together.

*We let him play with dolls,* Linda said. *He loves his dolls.*

I must have still been feeling sorry for her since I didn't rib her for the self-congratulatory tolerance. I must have been growing up, however belatedly, learning to not say what I thought or felt, no matter how urgently I thought or felt that thought or feeling, but on the drive home I regressed.

*Perhaps,* I began, unable to stop myself, *our emotionally distant father has something to do with the fact that Sarah is so eager to marry someone twenty years older than her? Has anyone ever thought of that?*

*Well, Sarah doesn't seem to be as affected by Dad.*

I didn't need to ask her where the comparative conjunction was pointing. We were quiet for a few moments in which she did seem to telepathically apologize. And I appreciated that. I'm not so cynical that I cannot appreciate such things. We were silent for some time.

*Why can't you just be happy for her?* Linda eventually asked.

*Why is being happy the only acceptable reaction to someone getting engaged? People marry the wrong people all the time and everyone has to act like—*

*You know what your problem is?* Linda was suddenly angry and put the car in park at a stop sign. *And it may hurt to hear this, but you're always saying you'd rather know the truth. Your problem is you think you're a man. I think that's really it—it would explain so much and—*

She stopped midsentence as three deer crossed in front of the car, two does and a buck. They paused, turned to look in the windshield as we looked out at them, and a sort of fog and pink light fell in the distance near some train tracks and a little broken shed. It was all too beautiful and too quiet to be real, not here, not in this world, the country part of this country.

I don't know what got into me or got out of me just then, but I opened my door, stepped out, moved toward the animals because I was thinking of that dead deer from so many years ago now, that life I ended, and I didn't want to cry in front of Linda, didn't want her to think I was crying about marriage, hers or mine or the platonic ideal of marriage, so I charged the deer, screamed at them, half hoping the buck would go wild and charge me, maim me with those antlers, with all those beautiful pounds of him, but they all darted away, leapt down the street, rounded a corner, and were gone.

# The Grand
# Claremont Hotel

*for Jesse Ball*

As the result of a clerical error, or what seemed to be a clerical error, I lived in room 807, an Economy Queen, on the eighth floor of the Grand Claremont Hotel, free of charge, for nineteen days.

As I was returning to the hotel on the final evening of my original reservation, a five-night business trip I had undertaken on behalf of The Company, the desk attendant handed me a pale beige envelope made of exquisite heavy paper, paper of such a high quality, such weight, that one might feel—whether correctly or incorrectly—that even by holding such an object one's life had just been irrevocably changed. The envelope had a matte navy lining and contained a heavy note card embossed with the Grand Claremont Hotel's official logo—a small illustration of the Grand Claremont Hotel's façade, encircled by an ornate typography reading *The Grand Claremont Hotel.*

In dark blue ink and intricate calligraphy, the note card read:

> *Due to Client Complaints*
> *The Company has no choice*
> *but to cease your employment.*

I stood in the lobby, briefcase at my feet, and read the note card several times, studying the tiny variations between each capital *C*—this loop a little wider, this one a little more narrow—counting and re-counting the syllables—it failed to be a haiku—and I wondered whether the speaker of this message had indicated which words were to be capitalized or whether the calligrapher had made such a decision on their own.

Stowing the note card and envelope in my overcoat's interior pocket, I thanked the desk attendant, took the elevator to the eighth floor, walked slowly to room 807, hung a DO NOT DISTURB sign on the exterior door handle, ingested a quantity of liquid from the mini-bar, and tucked myself into bed.

As I fell asleep—and I have always been an excellent sleeper, rarely if ever kept awake by fear or worry—I had a clear realization that, in all likelihood, I would never again enter Company Head-quarters, a building I had spent much time entering, exiting, and being inside. Indeed, each day of my life for the past twelve years had been defined by the hour I was expected to enter Company Head-quarters, how long I would need to remain within Company Headquarters, the tasks I would need to complete that day at Com-pany Headquarters, and the hour at which I could reasonably per-mit myself to exit Company Headquarters. On the days I was not expected to enter Company Headquarters, I was often abroad, meet-ing with clients on behalf of The Company. Upon completing these meetings, I had always returned to Company Headquarters to give reports on my travels, but now I had been informed that this pat-tern would go on no longer. What daily activities, I wondered, if anything, could replace my entrances and exits of Company Head-quarters, my service to The Company, the way in which The Com-pany had directed and used the hours of my life?

In my twelve years of employment at The Company, I had known other men who had been informed their labor was no longer needed by The Company.

Few had met this news peacefully.

One, some years ago, had cried out expletives and something about a sick wife that could be heard all over Company Headquarters before he was escorted from the building and never heard from again. Another had jumped off the roof of Company Headquarters—though the building isn't tall enough to cause significant damage, so he'd only ended up crushing both his legs. Another had simply gone home, gone to sleep, and never woken up again.

And now, wrapped in high-thread-count sheets and blankets, the use of which had been paid for by The Company, I had become one of these men for whom The Company had no use. This fact seemed to become a physical mass or a kind of pressure in room 807; I became aware of the subtle but undeniable sensation that I was being watched, as if my dismissal had been transfigured into an actual human being who stared at me as I fell asleep. Yet I also knew I was not being watched, that I was completely alone in the sumptuous folds of the Grand Claremont Hotel's luxury bedding. The mattress sucked me into itself in a way that was not at all reminiscent of my simple cot back at home, in the bare apartment I'd long kept for its affordable rate and proximity to Company Headquarters. I fell asleep with a perverse sense of comfort.

The next morning I awoke quite late in the day. Light slipped in at an angle. The curtain fluttered above an air vent.

I sat up in bed, propped a pillow between my back and the wall-mounted headboard. On the side table was a navy rotary phone, a lamp with a pleated navy shade, a Grand Claremont Hotel notepad, and a matching ballpoint pen with navy lettering along the shaft: *The Grand Claremont Hotel*. By the small window was a small chair. The walls were covered in thatched beige wallpaper.

I lifted the phone, dialed room service, ordered the Grand Claremont Club Sandwich with a side of fruit salad. The sandwich arrived a half hour later accompanied by a dill pickle spear unmentioned by the menu. I consumed this meal in bed, in full, in silence. I felt there was just no reason to leave room 807. I appreciated its beige-and-navy color scheme, its reassuring blankness. It was effective at its task—to be a room in which one could exist, gathering smells and washing them away, becoming weary and sleeping and becoming awake and becoming weary again. The four-by-four-foot shower collected nearly an inch of standing water, and though I realize this may be considered a plumbing defect, I appreciated this defectiveness as the shower's puddle gently softened the soles of my feet. The sink fixtures and cabinet pulls were ergonomic. The lighting was efficient and unromantic. Room 807 was remarkably unremarkable and yet I found so much in room 807 to remark upon, a paradox that amused me greatly, made me feel as if I had a deeply entwined understanding of room 807, as if room 807 and I were devoted siblings sharing a sly glance during Christmas breakfast as our father told some well-worn boyhood story that became more epic with each telling. We were irrefutably enmeshed. I loved room 807. I respected room 807's implacable roomness. No one could ever take the job of being a room away from this room, my dear room 807. I had no intrinsic motivation or desire to leave room 807, and if I ever did leave room 807, I realized, this would only be the result of someone else's insistence. I waited for the gentle knock of a housekeeper, perhaps a phone call warmly reminding me of the hotel's checkout policy, some kind of signal that the final moment of my stay at the Grand Claremont Hotel had come and my departure was, unfortunately, required and would also be greatly appreciated.

But there was no knock or call.

For three days I did not leave room 807, nor did I call room service, nor did I move unless absolutely necessary. I left the DO NOT DISTURB sign on the exterior doorknob and the sign did its job faithfully, guarding me from any manner of disturbance. Most of the time I lay in the stupefying and slightly perfumed bed. I felt beautifully empty, nothing more than a life. If I noticed a hunger or thirst, I consumed a cashew nut, a candied fruit, a gulp of faucet water. This is how I lived. This is what I became. At some point I even ceased to be waiting for a knock or call. I forgot what sound was.

On the third day, rested but somehow restless, I began to move the chair from its place by the window, into the bathroom, back to the window, to the bathroom and back to the window, a gentle labor, something to get through. I covered the television set with a sheet and placed the phone beneath the bed and moved the chair between window and bathroom until night, then tucked the chair into bed with me. We had been through so much. I slept well. So did the chair.

Late in the afternoon of my fourth day in room 807, I put my Grand Claremont Hotel bathrobe over my regular clothes, opened the door, walked down the hallway, filled my ice canister at the automated machine, made brief eye contact through an open doorway with a maid as she snapped a white sheet open above a queen bed identical to mine, then I returned to room 807. I stood at the door, seething with joy, ecstatic in my solitude and ecstatic for the solitude of others, far or near from me, contained in their other rooms, in their beds, in their bodies.

It was only four in the afternoon but I had a dry vermouth on ice, the last item from the minibar. I fell asleep quickly but awoke two hours later feeling bolder, as if I had just been reconstituted after some kind of total disintegration. I opened my door, removed the DO NOT DISTURB sign, and shut the door. I called room service and had them send up the Grand Claremont Steak Dinner Deluxe and a whole bottle of barley wine and that night I feasted with all the lights on, the curtains drawn back. I watched the people of that city

stroll the streets below me, move around in the windows of neigh-
boring buildings, and I felt I was almost speaking to all these people,
enduring beside them as all our lives ticked by. I waved at some of
them but none saw my wave, yet I believe they felt it. Yes, I believed
it was felt.

The next morning the ecstasy of my ice-machine journey and
meal and revelation had faded. I was staring into the mirror just for
the company when I heard several short door-knocks and *House-
keeping*, spoken in such a way you could almost call it singing. I went
to the door, opened it, and found the same maid I had seen in that
other room. She was considerably shorter than me but obviously more
powerful and efficient, the sort of person who could paint a whole
room without spilling a drip or taping the trim. Beside the maid
was a rolling cart tidily stocked with cleaners and tight stacks of
sheets and towels.

We smiled at each other, I think. At least she smiled. We remained
still. After some time I remembered what this was all about, that
this was the disturbance that I had allowed when I had revoked my
door-handle order to not be disturbed. The maid was the disturbance
of sudden order.

Leaving the door open, I walked across the room, took a seat in
the chair beside the window, and watched the city as she went about
her business. It seemed only a few minutes had passed when I heard
the maid say, *All done, goodbye*, in one breath, the door shutting
behind her. I turned to see room 807 made taut—my suitcase had
been moved to the closet and the sheet had been removed from the
television set and the telephone returned to its place beside the bed.
It was as if I had never been here. I felt like an entirely new person
in an entirely new room. I fell asleep that night in the chair. The
room remained pristine.

On the nineteenth day there was a knock at the door. It was a
slow, heavy knock—not the rapid tapping of a maid passing by—

a knock followed by a baritone voice projected through the door—
*I'm so sorry to be a bother, but may we speak for a moment?*

There had been, I was told, a gross oversight on the part of the
bookings department and I would need to vacate room 807 immediately. The man who told me this was wearing an immaculately
tailored suit the same reassuring shade of navy consistent among all
Grand Claremont Hotel paraphernalia. Everyone here at the Grand
Claremont Hotel, I was told, was deeply sorry for this inconvenience,
and they all sincerely hoped that I could forgive them; however, an
Exclusive King Room on the twentieth floor was ready for my
occupancy.

I thought of telling him that it was really quite all right, that I
should be moving along anyway, that perhaps nineteen days in the
Grand Claremont Hotel was enough days in the Grand Claremont
Hotel, but I also knew I had nowhere to be going, had no place that
required my return, had no people that were missing me.

*An Exclusive King Room would be quite fine*, I told the man in
the suit. He made an expression of elegant relief, and while escort-
ing me and my only suitcase to the twentieth floor he explained a
wedding party had booked the entire eighth floor and simply could
not be separated.

*It is entirely our fault, sir*, he said with a particular mix of dig-
nity and shame that only a man in such a fine suit can express. *We
do wish you a very fine stay at the Grand Claremont Hotel.*

My Exclusive King Room, room 2032, was much like my first
love, room 807, only everything was a little larger, every object seemed
to have a matching friend. The bed, of course, was wider and longer
and instead of two sham pillows there were three and instead of
one cylindrical reclining pillow there were two and instead of four
soft down pillows there were eight and all of them were much
larger than their counterparts down in room 807. The chair by the
window had a twin and between the two chairs was a low, round

table. The ceilings, I realized, were at least two feet higher than in room 807 and the window was thrice as wide. The window, upon closer inspection, was not only a window but also a door, a sliding door that permitted one to pass through it and stand on a narrow balcony.

Over the next few days in room 2032 I began to establish habits quite similar to those of room 807. Did I feel I was betraying my allegiance to room 807 by this new allegiance to room 2032? Indeed I did. But room 807 was getting married and didn't even think of me anymore. I was just trying to carry on. This is reasonable, I told myself, as I moved one of the chairs from the window to the bathroom to the window again, then switched chairs just to be fair, then moved that second chair to the bathroom, back to the window, and switched back to the original chair—well, this is just what you do in a room, in whatever room you find yourself within, and after all, I thought, the past is nothing. Once I worked for The Company and that means nothing now. It happens no longer. There is no way to spend any energy on the past. I am just here in this room. Walls. Chairs. Floor. Bed.

I was already beginning to forget room 807, forget what it had meant to me, forget the sensation of being within it. To forget something, to allow myself to forget something, this was somewhat extraordinary behavior for me as I am afflicted with deeply nostalgic proclivities, constant and pointless yearnings to reach back, always dragging my heels as the clock ticks. To begin to forget something, to even have the thought that the past is nothing—it all felt so radical I became immediately unrecognizable to myself. I once kept a beer-bottle cap for sixteen and a half years because it reminded me of the first good day of a good summer I spent mostly in a swimming hole that had a perfect rope swing, a memory I didn't want to release, a day I didn't want to let slip into the gnaw of forgetting, and now I had become, in an instant, a person who did not care about that bottle cap, about that day, about any feeling I'd ever felt that had faded into the past.

The past is nothing, I thought again. It felt cardiovascular. A steep hike. I went to sleep having this thought, dreamed of it, woke with it.

Each day, when the maid came, I excused myself to the balcony to give her privacy in her labor. There was no chair on the balcony, and there was barely any standing room, and as I stood there I would sometimes momentarily consider the option I had to lean across the rail far enough that gravity would just end me. But I never did. I somehow identified that as a choice not worth making, which meant I chose to keep living, which meant I chose to keep living in the Grand Claremont Hotel.

One day, when the maid came at her usual hour, I found it was raining rather heavily, so I remained inside room 2032, taking a seat in one of the chairs as she went about her routine. Not until she had almost finished her chores did I realize that I had been intently studying her every movement—the elongation and shortening of her limbs as she vacuumed, the militaristic precision of her bed-making method, her gloved finger searching for dust in the oddest of corners. It seemed the rigor of my attention had implied some sort of unintended message, because just before she left she lingered, looked at me, squinting a little, and said, *Anything else?*

A mix of coyness and fear and determination was in her voice. I didn't or maybe couldn't say anything. I must have been breathing heavily because I became critically aware of my lungs in my chest, a sort of pain and pressure in them, as if they were pushing on me from the inside, trying to get out.

She unbuttoned the top button of her shirt and I kept staring at her, still unsure of what she was trying to convey to me, or how my staring, a rather nonstandard and perhaps somewhat offensive behavior, had been interpreted to mean something when in fact it meant nothing at all. My inaction apparently gave her the signal to refasten her undone button and flee room 2032 with a cheerful *Goodbye!*

I am not altogether sure how long I lived in room 2032 but at some point a knock came, much like the knock that had ended my tenure in room 807. I was certain this would be the end of my stay at the Grand Claremont Hotel, yet I have been wrong about a great many facts in my life that I was, at one point, certain about.

*We are deeply sorry to trouble you*, the man in the navy suit said. The maid was standing just beside him, peering past me into room 2032. *But we have just learned that there will be some construction taking place on the roof of the Hawthorne Building, of which you have an excellent view, but we are afraid the noise and dust will cause too much of a disturbance to your days and nights and we really must insist upon a second relocation.*

I wanted to tell him that I was undisturbed by disturbance, that I no longer hung the DO NOT DISTURB sign on my door, and I also wanted to ask him if he knew why I was still here, and I wanted to say, to confess, really, that though I didn't object to living out all my foreseeable days in the Grand Claremont Hotel, I couldn't understand what had happened that had allowed me to remain here, and though I wanted to know what had transpired that made my tenure in the Grand Claremont Hotel possible, I also wasn't sure I wanted to know or could even stand to know the reasons I was still here. Maybe one shouldn't lift the hood of some machines. I said nothing, waited.

*We really must insist, sir, that you allow us to offer you more peaceful accommodations. An Executive Ultra-King Suite on the twenty-ninth floor is available for your occupancy. You needn't even pack up, as we will be happy to take care of that burden for you.*

At this the maid entered the room and began packing my meager things as the man in the suit guided me by the shoulder down the hallway to the elevator, up to the twenty-ninth floor, down the hallway and into the Executive Ultra-King Suite, room 2901, which was not just one but, in fact, four rooms: a sitting room with two sofas and one chair, a dining room with a large table, a bathroom with a tub you could nearly swim a lap in, and a bedroom containing a bed that was roughly the size of the entirety of room 807. Every room had large windows and the ceilings rose to such a height that I felt as if I were in a cathedral, or one of those opulent old banks built when dollars must have seemed more hopeful than they have turned out to be.

*This must be the finest accommodation in the entire hotel*, I said.

*We are so delighted you approve, sir.*

I wanted to ask the man in the suit where he lived, whether he had a room in the hotel, and if he did what did his room look like, and if he didn't, what did his home look like, and if he had a home and not a room did any other people share this home with him, and how did it feel to leave his home each morning to come here, to this building full of room-homes, temporary and semitemporary places for people who were on their way somewhere or lost along the way somewhere or people who did not fit into any category at all. But I said nothing to him, just felt a knot tighten in my gut, a knot in my throat, a knot in my head, as if I were a piece of rope meant to demonstrate how it's done—barrel knot, square knot, slipknot, and so on. At some point perhaps I may have known how to tie such things.

*Your luggage will be delivered shortly*, he said as he backed out the door, leaving me to the Executive Ultra-King Suite. *I don't wish to disturb you any further.*

Alone in the Executive Ultra-King Suite I could hear a slight drone, some sort of noise the suite had created, it seemed, by its own vastness. I walked from room to room, touched the various fabrics and surfaces—marble, stainless steel, linen, slate, hardwood, tile, sheepskin, bearskin, other kinds of skin, soft sheets, downy blankets, pillows, throw pillows, accent pillows, glass.

As the droning increased in volume, I wondered if I had missed some turn at some point in my life and now I was just passing through a series of spaces that had never been meant for me. The drone became even louder, that or my moroseness was having the best of me. No, I wouldn't let it, I thought. What I needed was a brisk walk, yes, in fact that was all I needed, though I also knew it was possible I might set out for this walk and never return. My skin went damp as this possibility began to seem more possible. The drone became louder. My bowels shifted like cargo on a storm-thrown ship.

I tried to steady myself against a nearby window and either my hand was trembling or the glass was trembling or everything was being shaken by the drone, and I wondered if somewhere in this room there might be a wild animal of which my body had become aware and was reacting biologically before I could react consciously. I looked all over all the rooms and found nothing save for the luxuries of the Executive Ultra-King Suite. The drone had reached such a volume I felt my teeth shaking in their gums.

I ran down the hallway and jumped into a waiting elevator, took that elevator to the lobby, but when I arrived in the lobby I was still on floor twenty-nine. I pressed the LOBBY key again. The doors shut and I believe I sensed the elevator move, yet when the doors opened again I was still on floor twenty-nine. I looked for additional instructions on how to operate the elevator but found none. I pressed LOBBY again, harder this time—I meant it. The elevator door shut and I was so sure I felt the elevator descend, that familiar sinking, but when the doors opened a third time I was still on the twenty-ninth floor.

Well, I am not one to allow such absurdity to continue. I won't let myself be made a fool. I went back to 2901, the suite, that special place. What is this? I asked myself, but even my own voice could not be heard over the drone.

What a person should remember at times like these, when all normalcy seems to have left you, is that all things begin and end in the mind. Anything can be in there and anything can be taken out—anything, any single thing, by which I mean everything can be taken out and whatever remains is what you are, not the sensations you feel, the food you eat, not the people you seem to know or the objects you own or the people you seem to own or the objects that have known you all your life. You're not even the memories you can remember or even the thoughts you can think. You are something below all those things. You are the little dog at the bottom of the pile; no, not even the dog but the smallest flea on the smallest dog at the bottom of the pile. Even less than that, even less and still somehow more than anything else—that's what you are. And when you can remember this everything becomes very still and you can move around easily, as if it were all a dream.

I noticed a door I'd overlooked upon my arrival to 2901, and opening it I found a large closet in which my few clothes had been hung, pressed. Also there were three navy suits and three white shirts monogrammed with the Grand Claremont Hotel logo. A navy telephone was mounted on the wall of the closet and as I stood there, awash in the drone, breathing the reassuring scent of clean laundry, the phone began to ring, and though I couldn't hear it over the drone a knuckle-size red light flashed to let me know.

As I lifted the phone to my ear the drone ceased, and I spoke that sad question—*Hello?*

*Good afternoon, sir, and how are you feeling today?*

I stood there with my mouth open.

*Is there anything else you need? Anything at all?*

I gathered myself to answer—*In fact, yes—I believe, perhaps, there is something wrong with the elevator.*

*And what, sir, might be wrong with the elevator?*

*Well, in fact, it seems to be stuck on this floor, won't allow me down to the lobby.*

*I don't understand, sir—*

*I got into the elevator here on the twenty-ninth floor intending to go down to the lobby so I might reach the street, and—*

*Technically*—the voice interrupted—*an elevator's job, by its very definition, is to elevate, and here at the Grand Claremont Hotel, our elevators do what they are defined to do.*

*Oh,* I said, unable to protest such an allegiance to words, *should I take the stairs down instead?*

*Sir, I must admit I am confused by your question. Is there anything else that you need?*

*That I need?*

*Yes—is there something unavailable to you on the twenty-ninth floor that you are trying to procure?*

*Well, I just thought I would go out for—*

*Out?*

*Out of the building, yes, into the street so that I could—*

*Sir, let's not be so hasty. There's no reason to take such drastic actions. We can have anything sent up that you might need or desire.*

*Well.*

*Is there anything else that you need or desire, sir?*

I may have forgotten what I needed, or perhaps forgotten what a need is, what a desire is, what the difference between these things might be, but eventually I came up with the closest thing I could manage to specifically want or need or desire—a removal.

*There's a noise in this room.*

*A noise, sir?*

*Yes, a kind of . . . humming. It's hard to describe. It started softly then became louder and louder, a kind of throbbing, even, though it*

*has stopped now, though I'm sure it's not gone, not really gone. It's re-*
*ally more of a feeling, actually, than a noise—*

But the line, I realized, had gone dead. I braced for the drone to
reemerge, but all that came was a knock at the door—one knock—
barely a knock at all. The man in the suit was there, all intent and
smiling.

*You've reported a noise, sir.*

How did you get up here?

*Sir?*

Did you take the elevator?

*Sir, I am here to attend to this issue of a noise. Would you mind if*
*I stepped into the suite to inspect this issue further?*

I stepped aside to let him in.

And will you take the elevator back down, to the lobby perhaps?

But he did not seem to hear my question or perhaps heard and
ignored me. I felt distracted by his suit and realized that I too was
wearing a suit like his. The maid came in, hurried past me to join
the man in the suit in the sitting room, who was squinting up at
each corner, staring into one then another, another. As the maid
passed me two strands of hair wafted from her head. One landed
on a shaggy white rug in front of me and the other on my left shoe.

For a few minutes, I felt unable to move. I stared down at those
two strands of hair, black and thick, and though I realize that technically hair is dead, they each seemed to be breathing, fluttering,
moving toward me, telling me something.

The man in the suit and the maid were looking around the
room, looking, it seemed, for the drone or whatever had caused
the drone. Some time passed in which they looked for the drone
and I stared down at these hair strands. At times I would look up
to see them examining something, tapping at the windows, peek-
ing under chair cushions, under rugs.

I imagined Company Headquarters going on without me, how my old cot was sleeping its object sleep without me. There were so many people in the world for whom The Company had no use. I shut my eyes. I knew it was not the end.

What I can say now is that the view from the Grand Claremont Penthouse is magnificent—I have always been humbled by the ocean. It has always worked easily on me. True, I cannot actually see the ocean from my window in the Grand Claremont Penthouse, for this is a landlocked country and the ocean is perhaps a thousand miles from us, but I can feel it in the air, somehow. I remember it still.

I stand at the window all day, watching my breath gather wet on the glass, fade, gather, and fade again. I do not bother moving the chair anymore. I am only slightly aware of putting food or water into myself. Sometimes I think of room 807, or 2032 or 2901—but more often I find myself fixed on the memory of those two strands of hair and what they told me about living and dying, but since there is only one thing to know about living and dying, I won't bother with it now.

# Acknowledgments

Jin Auh, Jessica Friedman, and the Wylie Agency; Emily Bell, Eric Chinski, and Farrar, Straus and Giroux; Anne Meadows and Granta Books; the Whiting Foundation; the English Department at the University of Montana; *Harper's Magazine, Granta, Oxford American, The Atlas Review, BOMB, Tin House, The Sewanee Review, Electric Literature, Das Mag,* and the *Virginia Quarterly Review*; Goose; and Jesse Ball, dearly, who bore and still bears many burdens.